"Would you plea

"Excuse me?" Alexan... heard him wrong. "...remove my bra."

"I did."

While she knew Roarke couldn't be making a pass at her with them imprisoned in the car's trunk, she didn't like the idea of removing her underwear—even in the dark. She had to force a calmness into her tone that she didn't feel. "Mind telling me why you want me to undress?"

As usual, Mr. Silver Tongue had an answer. "I want to push your bra out the taillight hole and use it as a flag."

"Couldn't we use your shirt?"

"Which article of clothing do you think will draw more attention?"

Dear Reader,

This holiday season, deck the halls with some of the most exciting names in romantic suspense: Anne Stuart *and* Gayle Wilson. These two award-winning authors have returned together to Harlequin Intrigue to reprise their much loved miniseries—CATSPAW and MEN OF MYSTERY—in a special 2-in-1 collection. *Night and Day* is a guaranteed keeper and the best stocking stuffer around!

Find out what happens when a single-dad secret agent has to protect a beautiful scientist as our MONTANA CONFIDENTIAL series continues with *Licensed To Marry* by Charlotte Douglas.

The *stork* is coming down the chimney this year, as Joanna Wayne begins a brand-new series of books set in the sultry South. Look for *Another Woman's Baby* this month and more HIDDEN PASSIONS books to come in the near future.

Also available from Harlequin Intrigue is the second title in Susan Kearney's HIDE AND SEEK trilogy. The search goes on in *Hidden Hearts*.

Happy holidays from all of us at Harlequin Intrigue.

Sincerely,

Denise O'Sullivan
Associate Senior Editor
Harlequin Intrigue

P.S.—Next month you can find *another* special holiday title—*A Woman with a Mystery* by B.J. Daniels

HIDDEN
HEARTS
SUSAN KEARNEY

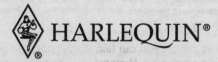

HARLEQUIN®

TORONTO • NEW YORK • LONDON
AMSTERDAM • PARIS • SYDNEY • HAMBURG
STOCKHOLM • ATHENS • TOKYO • MILAN • MADRID
PRAGUE • WARSAW • BUDAPEST • AUCKLAND

ISBN 0-373-22640-3

HIDDEN HEARTS

ABOUT THE AUTHOR

Susan Kearney used to set herself on fire four times a day. Now she does something really hot—she writes romantic suspense. While she no longer performs her signature fire dive (she's taken up figure skating), she never runs out of ideas for characters and plots. A business graduate from the University of Michigan, Susan is working on her fourteenth novel and writes full-time. She resides in a small town outside Tampa, Florida, with her husband and children and a spoiled Boston terrier.

Books by Susan Kearney

HARLEQUIN INTRIGUE

340—TARA'S CHILD
378—A BABY TO LOVE
410—LULLABY DECEPTION
428—SWEET DECEPTION
456—DECEIVING DADDY
478—PRIORITY MALE
552—A NIGHT WITHOUT END
586—CRADLE WILL ROCK*
590—LITTLE BOYS BLUE*
594—LULLABY AND GOODNIGHT*
636—THE HIDDEN YEARS†
640—HIDDEN HEARTS†

*The Sutton Babies
†Hide and Seek

Don't miss any of our special offers. Write to us at the following address for information on our newest releases.

Harlequin Reader Service
U.S.: 3010 Walden Ave., P.O. Box 1325, Buffalo, NY 14269
Canadian: P.O. Box 609, Fort Erie, Ont. L2A 5X3

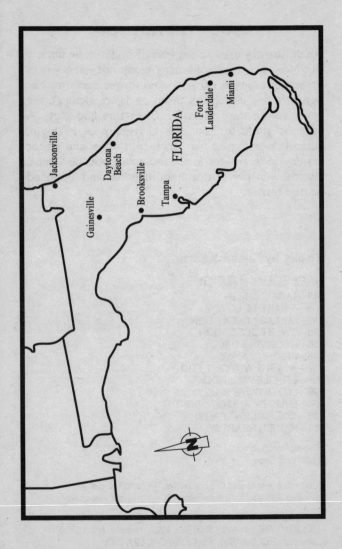

CAST OF CHARACTERS

Alexandra Golden—An architect, and a woman with a painful past. As she faces danger and Roarke's charm, can she find the courage to fall in love?

Roarke Stone—Charming, dangerous and sexy, the ex-CIA rogue is hired as Alexandra's bodyguard. He's determined to protect Alexandra, but will he succeed in protecting his heart?

Jake Cockran—The brother Alexandra never met. When Jake sends his sister a package from her biological parents, he inadvertently places her in danger.

Jake and Alexandra's biological parents—Letters, pictures and diaries—secrets from her mother and cloaked in a mystery that must be solved.

Carleton Jamison—An FBI agent who owes Roarke his life. He's one of the few men Roarke trusts.

Top Dog—Roarke's nickname for the bald man who wants Alexandra and her secrets.

Prologue

Alexandra Golden ignored the niggling worry that had shadowed her for the last two days. Ever since she'd received a package related to her mysterious past, she'd been fighting not to let it ruin her enjoyment of her latest accomplishment—a triumph she'd worked so hard to achieve.

With deep satisfaction and pride, Alexandra leaned over the finished blueprints of her architectural firm's first skyscraper. The two-hundred-story bank building overlooking the St. John's River in downtown Jacksonville, Florida, would boast majestic views of several bridges, the thriving waterfront and a good part of the bustling city. Best of all, it would be the first new construction project this decade to be added to Jacksonville's elegant skyline by a female architect.

As Alexandra smoothed her palm over the graceful lines of the beautiful bank building she would create out of soaring steel, solid concrete and cool-blue glass, she didn't regret one moment of the hard work she'd done to arrive at this moment. Just mastering the math required to become an architect had almost done her in, but she'd studied harder than many of her colleagues. Then she'd taken risks to establish her own firm, and she had even spread her finances to the limit to go after the Benson Bank project.

Early in her career, she'd made a friend. Charlotte Benson, heir to the Benson financial empire, had supported Alexandra's firm from the beginning. Charlotte had convinced her mostly male board of directors that a woman architect would help usher in the future, a future where women dropped off their children in day-care centers in the buildings where they worked. A future where women who opened their own businesses and sought financing from a bank would feel welcome. A future where widows could come in for investment counseling and trust their stock portfolios to the competent hands of Benson Securities's brokers.

So, with success at her fingertips, why couldn't Alexandra shake the feeling that something was wrong? She'd always been an optimistic person. She'd had her parents' full support ever since they'd adopted her, taking her from the foster home to live with them when she was three years old and too young to remember her past. She'd grown up loved and spoiled and encouraged to make her dreams happen. She had no bad memories of her former life and no recollections of a brother named Jake Cochran or the sister he'd claimed in his recent letter was just a baby when they'd all been separated.

At least Jake had had the good sense not to just show up on her doorstep. The arrival of his letter two days ago would let her prepare gradually for a meeting with him. And she did want to see what he was like; she wondered if he shared her dark hair, olive complexion and amber-colored eyes.

Jake's message to her had been brief, but warm in tone and friendly. So she had no reason to feel threatened because the brother she couldn't remember had sent her a note and a strange assortment of papers in the mail. He'd revealed nothing personal and had sent no photographs of himself. Instead he'd sent old black-and-white pictures from their parents' era and a copy of her mother's diary, along with birth certificates in a ten-by-fourteen-inch envelope. Alexandra had set the materials aside until she had time to go through them more carefully.

No reason to worry. So why was she tapping her short-clipped nails on the blueprints? Why couldn't she keep her mind on the present? Why did she keep glancing at the envelope she'd left on the dining-room table as if it contained a bomb?

The items inside looked harmless enough. Although she'd never had the time or inclination to brood over her past, she looked forward to meeting her siblings. But even if she'd remembered them, she didn't know if she would have tried to find them. Unlike many adoptees who yearned to seek out their genealogical roots, Alexandra had focused on her career and the parents who adored her.

She'd turned a page of the blueprints to look over the specs for the site layout and underground utilities when a knock on her front door interrupted her. Leaving the blueprints, she exited her home office and walked through the living room to her foyer.

As a single woman who lived alone, she habitually locked the dead bolt and chained the door after she arrived home. She'd never had trouble at the apartment complex, but she'd received a lot of publicity on the

Benson project recently. Her picture had been in the paper and she'd been interviewed on local television news. While the free promotion could prove a boon to her firm and make it easier to win more projects, she remained careful of strangers.

"Who is it?"

"Package service, ma'am."

Alexandra's packages were usually delivered to her office. But the one from her brother had come to her home. Perhaps he'd sent another?

Alexandra peered through the peephole. The short, middle-aged, clean-cut man with a wide chest wore an ill-fitting uniform and held a clipboard awkwardly in his meaty hands. But he held no package. Maybe he'd set it on the floor.

Alexandra opened her door but didn't unfasten the chain. "I wasn't expecting anything."

"I'm afraid there's been a mixup, ma'am."

Alexandra frowned. "What kind of mixup?"

"The package we delivered a few days ago isn't yours. If you could return it to me, we can deliver it to its rightful owner."

"Just a minute please."

Alexandra needed to think. She knew the package had her correct address and that if there had been a mix-up, the company would have called. But she'd received no phone call.

Something was wrong.

Her first thought was to phone the delivery company to check on what she felt was a bogus story.

"Ma'am, if you could open the door and give me the package, I can show you the wrong address on the label."

She knew the address was hers since she'd carefully checked it when it arrived. Her second thought was to get the hell out of her apartment.

"I'll be back in a second," Alexandra called over her shoulder, knowing the chain might not hold for long against a determined pounding, afraid that if she tried to shut the door and throw the dead bolt, he'd jam a foot in the doorway to prevent her from succeeding.

Heart racing, she sprinted through her living room, scooped up the envelope her brother had sent, ducked into her office and grabbed the blueprints and her purse.

The sound of the front door slamming open and the chain breaking the wood warned her that she hadn't a nanosecond to spare.

The man had just broken into her house!

Sweat slicking down her spine, Alexandra slid across her kitchen floor to her back door. As she juggled her belongings, she fumbled to turn the dead bolt.

The lock clicked open just as the deliveryman skidded into her kitchen. "Hold it right there, lady. I won't hurt you. I just need the package."

She didn't believe him. And she didn't stop running.

Yanking open the door, she rushed outside onto her second-story terrace.

She never doubted she would get away. Never expected to be caught.

But then she slammed into something hard.

Someone hard.

Strong masculine arms closed around her. Arms way too strong to fight.

Chapter One

Two men were after her.

A team.

Sent to take the package her brother had sent her.

Alexandra's first instinct had been to flee. Trapped in the big man's grip, she knew her only remaining option was to fight, take him by surprise.

But, unlike the short man in the sloppy uniform who had just slid and fallen with a loud thump, this man was tall, with shoulders as broad as the Panhandle and blue eyes that pierced like a laser. Eyes that seemed unfazed at finding her trying to flee.

Her head barely reached his chin, so slamming her brow into his face to escape wouldn't be an option. But she had no intention of giving up.

At least not without giving him her best shot.

Men may have evolved to be stronger than women, but that simply meant Alexandra had to be smarter. She slammed her foot down onto the big man's toe. He let out a grunt and one hand loosened its grip on her arm.

As he hopped in pain, she kicked his shin and

slapped his ear with the hand that still clasped her blueprints tightly.

She hoped he'd loosen the grip of his other hand on her shoulder. He did let go, but grabbed her by the waist with both hands, lifting her off her feet, bringing her up to eye level. "Woman, you hurt me."

She kicked. Missed. "Let me go—"

"Or?"

"I'll hurt you some more." She drew back her foot to kick him where it would really hurt. One good knee to the groin and he'd—

"Don't even think about it."

She'd made a mistake by warning him. He'd sensed her intention and twisted his hips so she lost the angle needed to wreak the most damage. She considered how much hurting she could cause by ramming her elbow into his chin.

Before she could put thought into action, the man in the uniform rushed out through the back door onto the terrace. He reached behind his back and pulled a gun. A big ugly gun with the muzzle pointed at her.

As icy fear sliced her, Alexandra's heart froze. She couldn't breathe, couldn't move.

The big man dropped her so fast she stumbled and fell to her knees. Suddenly, her opponent shifted his body between her and the guy in the uniform.

As if to protect her?

Confusion mixed with fear. Weren't the two men working together? Why had he let her go? Why would he place himself between her and his partner?

A shot fired and her ears rang. Burnt smoke singed her nostrils. Fear shook her legs. She expected to feel pain or to see the big man go down. Neither happened.

Her captor lunged and kicked the gun from the smaller man, then tackled him.

Alexandra still didn't understand why he'd let her go. She didn't understand why the pair were fighting. She didn't question her good fortune. Didn't stay around to ask questions. Without a backward glance, she fled down the stairs on watery knees. In her haste, she tripped and dropped her precious blueprints, which rolled onto the sidewalk and partially into the shrubs. She tugged on them and realized they'd snagged. They weren't worth her life. She kept running.

Above her she heard the sound of flesh smacking flesh, grunts, a groan of pain. A potted plant crashed onto the concrete patio beside her, the shards whizzing by her legs.

She raced around the apartment complex. Heard footsteps clanging down her terrace steps. Her heart jackhammering up into her throat, she sprinted toward the parking garage. She couldn't count on a neighbor hearing the shot and calling the police. She needed to escape now. If only she could make it to her car.

As she ran around the building's corner, she fumbled in her purse for her car keys. The steps behind were coming closer. He was catching her. She wasn't going to make it to her car and had only seconds to plan another course of action while her pursuer still couldn't see her.

The apartment building had been built on piers and pilings over the parking area. Two elevators provided access to the upper floors. In the middle of Monday afternoon, most people were at work. There weren't enough cars to hide behind, and she couldn't reach the next building or the woods behind the apartments before he caught up with her—whoever *he* was. Although she didn't know who had won the fight, she'd bet on the big man.

And she didn't want to take him on again. Kicking his shin had hurt her foot. Slapping his ear had stung her hand. He'd been one giant slab of solid muscle.

Looking around wildly for a hiding space, she saw the garbage Dumpster. Yanking open the lid, she ignored the awful smell, tossed her purse and her brother's envelope inside and scrambled over. She landed softly on her feet, making little noise. Her pursuer pounded around the corner just as she ducked out of sight.

She had no time to close the top. But if she had, the smell might have suffocated her. The Dumpster had been emptied recently and contained only a few tidy plastic garbage bags in one corner, a few rotting onions, rotten banana peels and maybe some decayed meat. She tried to convince herself that the odor wasn't so bad. The foul smell helped her control her ragged breathing as she tried to remain still, quiet.

If only she hadn't come home from work, but she'd needed a shower after inspecting the dusty job site. And then she'd gone over the plans again... Now she really needed a shower.

She held her breath as her pursuer walked past. She didn't dare peer over the side to see which man still pursued her. She didn't dare call out for help. In the middle of May, at the beginning of the week, the kids were still at school, their parents at work, the complex mostly empty.

And she'd left her cell phone in her car.

She heard the footsteps retreat and let out a quiet

sigh of relief. But then the steps returned, steady, measured steps. He was heading straight for the Dumpster, and her heart raced so hard, she thought it might burst through her ribs.

She crouched low next to the filthy side, ignoring the grease, old dirt and who knew how many billions of germs. When the big man peered inside and his eyes found hers, she expected to see anger or annoyance. She expected him to grab her. Shoot her.

But he chuckled.

Chuckled?

It was a deep chuckle without the least hint of malice. She didn't care how nice a chuckle he had, she backed up until her feet tripped up against the plastic bags.

Alexandra tried not to stare but couldn't help herself. When she'd been struggling in his grasp, she hadn't really looked at him. Now she saw that he was absolutely stunningly gorgeous, a fact she'd missed in her battle with him on her terrace. Terror alone could have made her unaware of his movie-star attractiveness as she'd fled from him earlier. This guy's face was the kind women fantasized over, and, naturally, the extraordinary face came packaged with a body worth dying for.

He smiled at her, and of course he had perfect teeth, too. And he knew it. His smile seemed to say come out, come out, I'm really one of the good guys.

"You can come out now."

Imagine that. He'd just told her she was safe—so naturally he expected her to believe it. If she hadn't been frightened half to death and partly mesmerized by his gorgeous good looks, she would have laughed as he actually put her thoughts into words. Naturally he had a deep, melodic knock-your-socks-off baritone to go with the rest of his perfection. Not once did she take her gaze from his face. Besides the bluest blue eyes she'd ever seen, he had an olive complexion, the kind that didn't require hours in the sun to tan, a straight aristocratic nose and gleaming white teeth. His black hair was cut short, neat and tidy over the ears. And he wore clothes as if he was born to model. A navy sports jacket emphasized broad shoulders, a white shirt accentuated his acre-sized chest, and khaki slacks, not the least bit rumpled from his fight, showed off slender hips. The only thing menacing about him, besides his huge size, was the five-o'clock shadow that underscored his tough-guy jaw.

"Look, I'm Roarke Stone. Didn't your brother tell you to expect me?"

His voice was as deep and non-threatening as his chuckle, but she didn't trust Mr. I'm-a-Good-Guy for a second. "My brother?"

"Jake Cochran."

"What about him?" She told herself not to let down her guard. Not to trust his seductive smile. Not to trust one thing he said just because he knew her brother's name. If he was after the envelope, like the intruder in her apartment, of course he would know her brother's name. And he'd try to feed her a line to convince her to hand it over.

He looked slightly puzzled but ready to smooth over her misconceptions. Oh so casually, he spoke. "Jake hired me to protect you."

Damn, he was good, coming up with a creative twist—one she hadn't expected. Still, she didn't believe him. And she couldn't quite believe his audacity either. He'd spoken with such conviction, as if he believed his own lies. Despite his charming good looks, those devastating blue eyes and the absolutely divine cheekbones, all she had to remember was how easily he'd lifted her off the ground, how easily he could hurt her, and she shivered.

Staying out of Roarke Stone's very long reach, Alexandra picked up her purse and the envelope she'd tossed into the Dumpster. Maybe if he had to jump inside to pursue her, she could climb out the other side before he grabbed her.

Meanwhile, her brain was thinking at warp speed. She'd keep him talking, distract him. "Who are you here to protect me from?"

"Maybe the man upstairs." His eyes narrowed at her accusingly. "Why did you let him into your apartment?"

Go figure. Now Mr. Perfection was trying to convince her *he* cared about her safety. Yeah right. But she played along. "Give me a little credit. The guy kicked in the door."

"What did he want?"

She couldn't believe she was standing inside a Dumpster having this unreal conversation with a man who looked as if he belonged in Hollywood, starring with Cameron Diaz. She noticed that despite the heat, he hadn't broken a sweat. He didn't seem to be breathing hard either, but his massive chest indicated he probably had the lung capacity of a distance runner or a marathon swimmer. However he was trying real hard not to breathe through his nose, and she didn't blame him. It really stank here, and she would dearly love to climb out of the Dumpster and take a three-hour shower—but not so much that she'd risk him grabbing her again.

She recalled how quickly he'd defeated the other man, how big his biceps were, how fast he'd moved and kept him at arm's length. Trying to refrain from glowering at him for displaying all that perfection which she was supposed to find irresistible, she attempted to clear up her confusion. "You weren't working with the man in the uniform?"

Roarke shook his head and smiled that sexy smile again. "I already told you. Your brother hired me."

His smile bounced right off her. "You can't be serious. And I suppose Jake wants back the stuff he sent me?" she muttered sarcastically, failing to believe this wasn't simply another ruse to persuade her to turn over the envelope to him. But what could be so valuable about the envelope's contents that her brother thought she needed protection?

He shot her a look loaded with reasonableness. "Jake didn't mention wanting anything back. He feared he might have inadvertently put you in danger."

Don't believe him. No matter how he smiled at her, Roarke Stone—if that was his real name—was making up a story, trying to coax her into trusting him so she'd give him the envelope. Mr. Perfection could take his charms and sell them elsewhere. She wasn't buying his explanation. Wouldn't her brother have called *her* if he'd thought she needed protection? It seemed rather extreme to hire her a bodyguard without even talking to her first. Of course, she hadn't been home much since she'd been working over eighty hours a week on the new project, but Jake could have left a message at her office.

If he had the number. She didn't have any idea if her brother knew what she did for a living or if he knew where she worked.

Roarke reached into his back pocket, pulled out a wallet and extracted a business card. She refused to step forward to take it.

He looked surprised and shocked and a tiny bit hurt at her obvious reluctance to believe him. "I can think of much more pleasant places to have this conversation."

She was sure he could. This guy was too much. But he was so good that she almost believed him. However, she had absolutely no intention of going anywhere more pleasant with him. Not now. Not ever.

"I see no reason to talk to you at all." Alexandra ignored the slight flush on his face as he stewed over her rejection, as if this was the first time a woman had ever turned him down. He looked so uncomfortable she almost felt sorry for him. Almost. "Why don't you just turn around and go back to wherever you came from?"

"I'd like to, but I'm afraid I've already been paid." A flash of amusement at her predicament and something else, maybe guilt, flickered in Roarke's blue eyes. "Besides, I do have a business reputation to maintain."

Without waiting for her reply, he bent and straightened, picking something up off the pavement. When he raised his hand higher than the lip of the Dumpster, she could see he held the blueprints she'd dropped.

"I thought these plans might be important to you. Are these papers why that man was after you?"

Alexandra uttered a very unladylike word. She'd been hoping to return to where she'd dropped her precious blueprints and recover them. Now he'd ruined that plan, too.

When he offered her the blueprints, she scampered over the edge of the Dumpster's far side. Roarke made no move to pursue her. Instead he offered the blueprints again, that half-puzzled, half-hurt expression he did so well trying to convince her he was harmless.

When she stayed away, he shrugged. "Can't say I blame you. I wouldn't want bits of garbage all over them either. But then again, I wouldn't want that man upstairs gaining free access to my apartment."

Alexandra knew better than to return to her apartment where the other man could be waiting for her. What she wanted was to go to her car, use her cell phone and call the police. Keeping the Dumpster between them, she watched Roarke warily, hoping she might distract him enough so she could make it to her car.

As if sensing how much she distrusted him, he held up his hands and backed away another foot or two. "Don't worry. I don't intend to come any closer than I have to." But he kept smiling confidently at her. A perfect smile. An interested smile. An...interested smile?

By the way he scrunched up his nose, she knew she smelled. And it just went to show how fake his offer had been when he'd suggested going somewhere pleasant to talk since he'd made it while she stank just as badly as she did right now. And if she smelled so bad, that smile plastered on his face that indicated interest was likely forced. Fake.

Mentally, she rolled her eyes. As if she'd ever believe Mr. Perfect would consider her even a remote candidate for pleasant conversation. "If you hadn't chased me, I wouldn't have had to climb in there."

"I needed to make sure no one else was waiting for you downstairs."

Yeah, sure. He cared about her safety. Uh-huh. She edged slowly toward her car, asking questions and somehow knowing he'd have a perfectly logical and innocent-sounding answer no matter what she asked. "What were you doing on my terrace?"

"The man at your front door didn't look like any delivery man I'd ever seen."

She strolled toward her car, and he maintained a good eight feet of distance from her. "What do you mean?"

"How many delivery guys can afford a Rolex watch and Air Jordan sneakers? His jacket bulged as if he was carrying a weapon. And he drove a rented Saturn instead of a truck."

More lies? Or was Roarke Stone really that observant? It didn't seem fair that the perfect face and magnificent body should have a working brain behind them to boot.

She kept walking toward her car, keys in her hand. "You still haven't explained why you were on my back stoop."

"Instinct."

"What do you mean?" Casually, she unlocked her car, hoping to slip inside and lock it before Roarke prevented her from escaping.

"I figured if you were home, the man was trouble. It seemed likely you might try and leave out the back—just like you're trying to abandon me now." Roarke advanced, leaned inside and plucked her cell phone from the cradle and held it up. "Instinct. This what you're looking for?"

Damn his instincts. She'd almost relaxed, thought he'd been relaxed, too. He was that good. She realized her mistake after he'd taken away her phone with lightning speed, moving too fast for her to block him.

Fear came back, sinking and swooping in her stomach. "I need to report the break-in to the cops."

"Why?"

"Well, duh! So they can catch him."

"That's an admirable idea but a naive one." He crossed his arms over his chest. "But it's my job to protect you, and I can do that better without the local authorities interfering."

She didn't like the way his eyes had gone from calm to stormy, making her feel as though she was barely keeping her head above high seas. "You can protect me better than the police?"

"Absolutely."

His self-assurance pumped another jolt of fear into her veins. This couldn't be happening to her.

"I suggest we return to your apartment. Together."

Together? She didn't like the purposeful look in his eyes. Eyes that expected her to melt simply because they focused on her. And why would he take her back there? She started to back away. When he moved, he acted with a blur of speed, bracketing her wrist with his hand before she'd had a chance to jerk back.

She tugged, but might as well have tried to move a front-end loader. "Let go."

"No can do. I'm responsible for you now."

Sure he was. She didn't like the sound of that self-confident declaration one bit. It was too take-charge, too commanding and way too macho, reminding her of another man in her past, one who'd hurt her badly.

Roarke tugged her gently away from her car. She stiffened her legs and almost fell on her face as he dragged her forward, her resistance futile.

Suddenly he stopped, and she almost ran into him. Roarke's incredible patience seemed to be running out. He grimaced with distaste at her smell. Right now she was very glad she smelled, because the last thing she wanted was for this too-perfect man to find her attractive in any way.

His charming tone now held an edge. "This would be easier if you cooperated."

"Cooperate?" She didn't bother to hide her growing panic. Didn't care that he looked truly sorry for causing her fear. If he didn't want her to be scared, he could let her go. "Am I supposed to read your mind and know where we're going? Am I supposed to know which way you intend to tug me and when?" She didn't want to go anywhere. Especially to her apartment.

Especially with Roarke Stone.

Chapter Two

Alexandra glanced sideways at Roarke and wondered how to persuade him to head anywhere but back upstairs. Clearly, the man was used to getting his own way.

But she needed to stay in public view. Sooner or later, someone might come by, someone she could call to for help. Or maybe calling for help wouldn't be believable—not if anyone came close enough to see Roarke's too-handsome face. Maybe she should yell Fire.

Roarke seemed oblivious to the possibility of rescue. He stood calmly, supremely confident that everything would go his way. Yet when she looked more closely she noted that despite the stillness of his head, his eyes scanned from side to side as he half-led, half-pulled her around the building and out into the sunlight.

The big jerk. If she wouldn't cooperate, he'd use force. No problem seemed to deter him. Alexandra gasped and yanked him to a halt.

"Now what?" Roarke sounded as though he suspected she was up to mischief.

If he was a bodyguard, which she still very much doubted, he wasn't taking her situation seriously enough to suit her. But he seemed just too handsome and too supremely confident to be a bad guy. Alexandra had to remind herself that Ted Bundy had looked handsome throughout the trial in which he was convicted of killing several coeds. He'd looked good right up to the day the State of Florida had fried him in Old Sparky, the electric chair. Good looks had nothing to do with morals or whether one chose to be a criminal. Neither did confidence. Or arrogance.

She really didn't like Roarke Stone. She didn't like the way he assumed she would go along with whatever he said. She didn't like the way he used his smile to try to convince her he was a good guy. And she especially didn't like the way her pulse quickened at his extraordinary looks and kept making her forget how dangerous he could be.

Still, if she had to be manhandled, she preferred Roarke to the man he'd fought upstairs. The man who might have recovered and might even now be waiting for them to return. "That man might still be up there."

"Don't worry about him. He's long gone." Roarke didn't blink one long black eyelash at her suggestion that they might be about to walk into danger. He tugged her along the sidewalk toward the steps leading up to her terrace.

"You can't know he left," she insisted, knowing that trying to change Roarke's one-track mind was probably futile.

"I saw him drive away in his Saturn while you were in the Dumpster."

Ha! She'd caught him. "So you lied to me when you said he was upstairs ransacking my apartment?"

"I said I wouldn't want that man upstairs having free access to my apartment." He repeated his earlier words exactly. He didn't even bother with a sheepish grin when he added, "I didn't say he was there."

But he'd implied it. And his excuse seemed too convenient. Roarke must have been born with a remarkable memory to recall his own words with robotic precision. Only there was nothing robotic about the way his eyes lit up with desire when he glanced her way. Nothing robotic about the way her tummy fluttered in response.

Alexandra had met several men like him during her career. Smart. Good-looking. Self-assured. Unfortunately, one was a past boyfriend. And she'd learned not to trust a word Patrick said.

Her ex-lover had been so convincing that she'd often wondered if he had believed his own distortions of the truth. He'd been too handsome for her good— just like Roarke. She'd been naive back then. Before she'd realized that his gorgeous face hid a rotten character, he'd broken her heart. She'd learned a lesson she hadn't forgotten.

If she could just keep Roarke spinning his tall tales, surely someone would come along soon. Someone who would notice she wasn't willingly walking alongside him. Someone who would call the fire department when she shouted. But she didn't yell yet, waiting for the right moment when she'd spy one of her neighbors, knowing she might only have one chance.

She tried to keep her tone conversational. As if every day strange men pulled her along the sidewalk with them. "Why didn't you go after the man who broke into my apartment?"

"My job is to protect you."

"Well, I'd feel a lot more protected if the bad guy was in jail instead of driving away." Her words might be sarcastic, but in truth, she was starting to shake inside. Since she rarely came home during office hours, she hadn't realized just how deserted the apartments were during the day. Not a curtain moved. No kids played outside.

He spoke with a confidence that didn't reassure her. "I have the license-plate number."

"You do?" If he'd written that down, it would help her believe he really was a bodyguard sent by her brother to protect her. Her hopes rose a notch. Surely she couldn't be lucky enough for this guy to be legitimate. "Let's see the number. We can call it in to the cops and let them trace it. They might lock the guy up before lunchtime."

"First of all, I didn't have time to write down anything." Her hopes plummeted. With his free hand, he pointed to his temple. "I memorized the number and letter combination. And second, you have unfounded faith in a police department that's overworked and underpaid. Have you ever reported a crime?"

"My car was stolen once." It had taken the officers hours to come out and take her statement.

"And?"

"They found it."

"How long did it take?"

"Three months," she admitted, wondering how else she could stall. "If my brother Jake really hired you, tell me what he looks like."

Roarke couldn't know she'd never seen a picture of Jake.

"I accepted the job over the telephone."

Damn! He had an answer for everything. Maybe he was telling the truth. He had fought off that other man. He had placed his body between her and the gun aimed at her. Yet, wouldn't a bodyguard welcome help from the local authorities, not avoid it?

When he'd offered her back her blueprints, her suspicions had abated. She knew such a small gesture shouldn't weigh so heavily in his favor. And yet, a criminal wouldn't be so considerate, would he? Would a criminal have stopped and explained as Roarke had just done?

Maybe—if her cooperation would make it easier for him to get her back into her apartment...where she would be alone with him.

She couldn't make up her mind. If Roarke Stone was really a bodyguard, why would he want her to return to her apartment where she could so easily be found? She shook her head as once again he tugged her toward the stairs leading to her back terrace.

Again she halted. "Why are you so insistent on taking me back to my apartment?"

"You need a shower."

"A shower?"

No way was she about to take off her clothes with him around. Not in a million years. She wouldn't trust a locked door. With shoulders like his, he could break through in an instant. And she just knew from the determined look in those baby blues glinting with amusement that he had no intention of leaving her alone.

"Lady, you reek."

She'd always objected to being called lady, or woman. As though she wasn't an individual with her own name. Besides she wanted this man to think of her as a person with her own life. He might be less inclined to hurt her if she didn't act like a nameless victim.

"My name's Alexandra."

"Fine, Alexandra. You stink, and client or not, I refuse to be around anyone who smells as bad as you do."

While she couldn't refute the truth of his statement, she hesitated. Removing her clothes while he stood outside her door still wasn't a viable option. She'd be way too vulnerable.

Pretending she believed his story about being there to protect her was the best way to deal with Roarke. She tried to calm her leaping nerves. "We shouldn't go back up there. He might have left, but he could return."

"I won't leave you alone."

"He might bring a friend."

"I'm prepared for that contingency."

Always prepared—just like a Boy Scout. Except he didn't look at her like any boy she'd ever known. He focused on her with an unnerving intensity that made her shiver. Exactly what she'd been afraid of.

She needed to come up with an alternative plan. No way was she going to suggest getting into a car with this stranger. If he insisted on holding her captive, she was better off where someone might hear her scream. Such a sobering thought gave her the confidence to look him straight in the eye with a boldness she was far from feeling.

"You can't expect me to shower with a strange man in my home."

"Why not?"

"Because I won't."

"Lady—"

"Alexandra."

"Alexandra, do you like the way you smell?"

Of course she didn't. But that was the point. As long as she wore garbage like perfume, no man would find her attractive. Not even a criminal. The stench protected her. The stench protected her from him.

She cocked her head to the side, pretending to be puzzled and hurt by his accusation. "What smell?"

Roarke's very male, very hard lower jaw dropped in astonishment and then he chuckled again, the same deep chuckle that had thawed her before and made her consider whether she could trust him.

"Nice try, la—Alexandra," he corrected himself, definite amusement lighting up his face. "You *will* take a shower. But I'll give you a choice."

She didn't like the sound of his statement since it sounded too much like an ultimatum. Then again, she had little alternative but to stand here and listen while his hand manacled her wrist like steel.

"You either shower by yourself, or, I'll climb in with you and do the honors myself."

ALEXANDRA HAD NEVER heard such a harsh ultimatum sugar-coated with such silky seductive charm. What kind of man was Roarke Stone? Obviously one who didn't take no for an answer. Obviously one used to women giving in to his every whim. Obviously one who believed she should obey his every command.

As she trudged beside him up to her apartment, she didn't bother wasting her energy trying to fight him again. He'd disabled an opponent much stronger than her in less than sixty seconds, and all she would accomplish by using the few basic self-defense skills she knew was to hurt herself.

Although Roarke hadn't struck her when she'd attacked him the first time but had simply overpowered her with brute force, she couldn't take a chance that he might lose his temper and knock her out if she defied him again. While he didn't seem the type to strike a woman, he certainly had demonstrated his ability to boss her around.

He was arrogant. Conceited. And he wanted her to get naked while he was in her apartment.

Patience. She needed to wait for a better opportunity to escape. Besides, she'd think better and move more quickly if she remained uninjured.

The hard part was going to be matching wits with her captor. He'd not only shown her that he commanded great strength, but he possessed a remarkable memory for details. And he had an uncanny ability to anticipate what she was about to do before she did it—as when he'd moved his thigh to prevent her landing a knee to his groin and when he'd plucked her cell phone from the cradle in her car.

He'd also come up with a rational explanation for her every objection. And he'd carefully told her things she couldn't check out while he remained with her. With incredible perception, he'd known exactly what to say to make her doubt her doubts about him. If she wasn't careful to guard her thoughts, she'd start exhibiting that Stockholm syndrome where a kidnap victim begins to identify with her captor.

Luckily she knew she could never again fall for this type of charm or lies. Let him do his worst. He could turn up the heat all he wanted and she wouldn't respond. After being struck once by his particular kind of good looks and charm, she was now immune.

But if she wasn't careful, she'd soon have herself believing he could read her mind. While he wasn't allknowing and all-powerful, he clearly was a man used to giving orders and getting his own way.

She had no doubt he would follow her into the shower if she protested again. So she didn't.

When he pulled out a shiny black gun, she restrained a gasp and managed to remain quiet as he pointed it toward her apartment—not her. Clearly the weapon was a precaution to ensure their safety as he checked every room and closet to make sure they were alone.

He moved quickly, quietly, seemingly taking no interest in her pictures of family in the dining room. Likewise, he spent no time looking at her framed design awards hanging in the hall. He didn't slow as they passed her expensive computer or stereo system. Roarke seemed solely focused on places where someone could hide, but whether his desire was to protect her or himself, she had no way of guessing.

Without talking, he'd also made another point. No way would she attempt to fight a man holding a weapon as handily as he did. He handled the gun, casually, expertly. The weapon seemed an extension of his body.

"It's clear." He tucked the gun back into a shoulder holster he wore under his loose-fitting jacket. "Gather up some clothes. Go take a shower. Lock the door if it'll make you feel safer. Meanwhile, I'll bolt the front door."

He released her hand but nonchalantly blocked any possible escape. She hurried into her bedroom, hoping he wouldn't follow her, and let out a small sigh of relief when he didn't.

She supposed not many women would run away from a man that good-looking. In fact, she was counting on it, hoping he wouldn't anticipate her next move.

She glanced longingly at the portable phone and decided not to risk it as she heard the bolt on her front door drive home. While she might dial 911 before he stopped her, it would take the police several minutes to arrive. She could be dead by then.

Rather than let that grave thought deter her, she worked faster. She snatched up a plastic shopping bag and dumped out the shoes she'd bought last week. Quickly she snatched the top sheet off her bed and stuffed it into the shopping bag, then she floated the coverlet back over the bed to hide the missing sheet in case Roarke got curious and ducked in for a look. Finally she grabbed a change of clothing and stuffed it on top of the sheet.

She returned to the hallway a little breathless, hoping she hadn't taken too long and aroused his suspicions. Roarke had angled a chair so he could watch the front and back entrances to her apartment as well as the short hallway from bedroom to bathroom.

Without meeting his eyes for fear he'd guess her intention, she hurried into the bathroom. As soon as she closed the door behind her, Alexandra dumped the clothing on the floor. Quickly she tied one end of the sheet to the towel bar. Praying the bar would remained attached to the wall and would hold her weight, she tugged hard.

The knot held.

She turned on the shower. The water would disguise any noise she made opening the window. She closed the toilet seat, climbed on top and threw the end of the sheet out the open window. Although the sheet wouldn't reach the ground, she believed she could drop safely to the grass when she reached the sheet's end.

She didn't allow herself the luxury of thinking how surprised Roarke would be to find her gone. Palms sweaty with a combination of fear of discovery and fear of dropping out of a second-story window, she placed one leg through the window and started to ease herself through.

The bathroom door opened.

Alexandra froze, her hands on the sheet, still half inside the bathroom.

He took in the dumped clothes, the sheet and her awkward position in one quick but thorough glance and let out a long, low whistle. "Going somewhere?"

"How did you—"

"Know?" He lifted one insolent eyebrow. "You didn't lock the bathroom door."

"Huh?"

In one swift move, Roarke tugged on the sheet and pulled her into the bathroom, backing away as he got a good whiff of her odor. "As nervous as you were about taking your clothes off around me, if you'd intended to take a real shower, you would have locked the door.''

Damn him. Damn his know-it-all-superior grin. Damn his mind that didn't overlook a detail. Damn him for the glimmer of respect she'd read in his eyes.

How did he already know her well enough to predict her actions? Could he have been stalking her for weeks? She'd read about some weirdo stalkers who weren't ex-boyfriends but simply casual acquaintances who fixated on a woman for no logical reason. Could she have seen this man at the bank? At work? On a construction site?

Ignoring her completely, he untied the sheet and tossed it into the hallway. He took one last efficient look around the bathroom, peering through the tempered-glass shower doors as if searching for any other means of escape. He must have decided she was trapped and walked out.

In frustration she kicked the door shut behind him and viciously twisted the lock. When it clicked, she heard his disturbing chuckle.

She supposed she should count herself lucky that he hadn't followed through on his threat to stay in the shower with her. He could have…

Better not to think about what he could have done. With those large hands and powerful arms he could do just about anything he wanted.

She was wasting hot water. But did she dare get naked even with a locked door between them?

Why not? If he wanted to remove her clothes he could already have done so. But maybe he was just waiting until she washed away the awful smell.

She sensed that he was capable of violence. And

yet…he seemed more amused by her defiance than angered. Almost as if he respected her ingenuity.

A look in the mirror made up her mind. Her hair had escaped the neat French braid and something dark and sticky oozed at her temple. Several smudges stuck to her cheek and chin. And her blouse and slacks were filthy. Knowing she'd never wear them again, she stripped, tossed the soiled clothing into the plastic trash-can liner and tied a knot to keep down the odor.

Within seconds she ducked into the steamy shower, her hands reaching for the soap. With resignation, she realized she could no longer fight Roarke's wishes as well as her own. She longed to feel clean. Besides, she rationalized, even if she managed to escape Roarke, no one would help her if she looked like a bag lady.

Alexandra wanted to take a quick shower, but once she stepped under the glorious flow of water, she decided that if Roarke Stone had violent intentions towards her, a longer shower wouldn't make that much difference. If she was going to wash away some of the stench that might have protected her, she might as well wash away all of it.

She soaped down, rinsed and soaped again. Next she attacked her hair, using double her normal amount of shampoo and letting it soak as she washed herself squeaky clean.

Besides, how could she think clearly when she stank? Every time she'd turned her head another awful smell had assaulted her, distracted her. And Roarke might listen to her if she changed her appearance. If she looked respectable, then maybe he'd treat her with respect.

Not that he'd mistreated her—if she didn't count forcing her to take a shower and taking away her cell phone, her only means to call for help. But why didn't she sense any real menace in him? Because he treated her gently? Because she'd seen amusement in his eyes when she'd expected anger?

Alexandra rinsed her hair, applied conditioner and gave her underarms and legs a quick swipe of the razor. The soothing routine lifted her spirits. When she finished, she brought a few locks forward to her nose and sniffed.

All clean.

She dried herself and dressed in fresh underwear, blue jeans and a shirt, before quickly rebraiding her hair. Her fingers worked smoothly, easing the wet strands off her face and working her hair into the braid until she fastened it all with one scrunchy at the back of her neck.

She brushed her teeth and applied moisturizer to her skin before she realized she was stalling. While Roarke hadn't interrupted her, giving her the privacy she so desperately needed, she dreaded dealing with him again.

Hating the uncertainty of whether he was friend or foe, she vowed to try and clear that matter up first, before she made any other decisions about her predicament. But what would make her believe him? Even if he allowed her to call her brother and Jake confirmed that he'd hired Roarke, how would she know that the other man on the phone was really her brother?

She and Jake had never met. At least not since she was three and he was five years old.

And even if Jake was her brother, how could she know if he was being honest with her? Brother or not, he could be some kind of con man with his own agenda. But what kind of swindle could anyone try to pull on her?

She wasn't wealthy. She could think of nothing she owned that anyone would want. Which made her think that Roarke Stone might be who he said he was—someone hired by her brother to protect her. He had saved her from the man in the uniform...unless they were playing good guy/bad guy so she would trust Roarke. Now her thoughts were really flying out there.

She had to pull herself together mentally as well as physically. And she could only do that by admitting the truth to herself. Roarke Stone reminded her of her painful past. A past where another man's good looks, easy smile and charm had betrayed her. She found Roarke's self-confidence alarming. And even worse, she wasn't quite as immune to him as she would have liked.

Apparently Patrick hadn't done the number on her she'd thought. Or she'd recovered enough to once again find herself reacting to certain traits. What was wrong with her that the only men she found attractive were the ones who couldn't be trusted?

Giving herself a good talking to had only made matters worse. Now she had not only to escape from Roarke but from her own thoughts about him.

A soft knock startled her. "You about done? We should be moving out."

Moving out? Was that an army term?

"Almost ready." She unlocked the door with a deep breath and faced him.

He stood so close that she had to force herself not to retreat. She hadn't expected him almost to overwhelm her simply by occupying the space around him so completely. Nor did she expect a head-to-toe inspection as if she needed to pass muster.

He nodded slightly, and she realized he'd been holding his breath. Slowly he sniffed and the tightness around his mouth eased.

"Ah, much better. Pack some clothes and toiletries, we need to clear out."

She should have been offended, but how could she be when she had smelled so awful? Besides, she might obtain more information if she once again pretended to cooperate. "And where are we going?"

"I've been thinking it over. What do you think about heading to Amelia Island?"

He'd just asked her opinion, so she decided not to point out that he still stood much too close. Maybe he hadn't noticed that he was close enough to hear her ragged breathing and smell her fear. Only now her fear wasn't over her own safety, so much as her reaction to him. She didn't want to notice this man's masculinity. But how could she not with his broad chest and tanned throat less than twelve inches from her face? She was close enough to see soft swirls of dark chest hair peeking out from beneath the V of his shirt. For the first time, she could breathe in his scent—none. He must use odorless shampoo and deodorant and no cologne.

"You look good," he told her in his too-sexy voice.

Not as good as you. "Thanks." She played along, pretending to accept the compliment she knew was insincere. She'd bet her blueprints that this man dated women of super-model beauty. She'd bet her bank contract the last woman in his bed had breasts that overflowed his large hands. She'd bet he was simply trying to manipulate her into doing something else she didn't want to do. But she could handle it since she understood the game.

His five-o'clock shadow was sexy as sin, as was the way he focused all his attention on her with warm approval.

She gave herself a mental shake and recalled that he'd just asked her a question about Amelia Island, a popular resort just north of Jacksonville, and she had yet to respond. "You want to go to Amelia Island?"

"I meant the Caribbean Islands."

He wanted to take her out of the country? "You can't be serious."

But that was a dumb thing to say. She could see by the upward lift of his eyebrow that he was dead serious.

"I don't have a passport."

"You only need a birth certificate."

"Look, my work is at a very delicate stage. And while you think I'm in danger—"

"Your brother's a private investigator. I don't think he'd have hired me if you weren't in some kind of trouble." Roarke stepped back enough for her to exit the bathroom. His massive shoulders almost touched both walls of her narrow hall, leaving her only enough room to head toward her bedroom. "The best way for me to protect you is to hide you someplace where you would never go."

"The Caribbean Islands are out of the question—

not unless you drug me and carry me onto the plane, and then someone might be suspicious.''

''Be reasonable, Alexandra.''

''Reasonable?'' She placed her hands on her hips and spun to face him. ''You want reasonable? How about the fact that I signed a contract to oversee the construction of a skyscraper that is going to be the finest building south of the Mason-Dixon line? How about the fact that work will stop if I don't show up tomorrow? How about the fact that everything I've worked my whole life to achieve will be ruined if I go off and hide in the islands with you?''

''And how about,'' he threw her own words back at her, ''that you're risking your life to stay here?''

''There's a major inspection of the building coming up in a few days. I have to be there—''

''I thought architects drew up plans. Why do you have to go to the site?''

''Designing the blueprints is only one part of my job. I've been hired to oversee the project to ensure the contractors adhere to my design specifications. And to do that, I have to be there when the city inspectors—''

''Look, that man came to your house, he likely knows where you work.''

''And if it's your job to protect me, then it'll be up to you to figure out a way to keep me safe,'' she insisted.

''I'm not a miracle worker. The best way to keep you safe is to hide.''

''No can do. I designed that building with clean lines and graceful curves, so people would have better places to work. If I miss the inspections, some man may think the day-care center isn't necessary and turn it into an exercise room.''

''Is the building more important than your life? Are you determined to end up dead?''

Chapter Three

Alexandra sank onto the bed and dropped her face into her hands. Some things were worth dying for: protecting a loved one; fighting for a just cause; defending one's homeland. But an inanimate object such as her beautiful skyscraper wasn't worth her life.

And yet, Roarke could be blowing matters out of proportion to make her more malleable. When he couldn't sweet-talk her into doing what he'd wanted, he'd changed tactics. He gone from charming to take-charge so fast that her thoughts spun. And he sounded so sure she was putting her life at risk that he'd almost convinced her. Almost.

Yet, the man who'd broken through her front door had only wanted the envelope Jake sent her. He'd specifically said he wouldn't hurt her. She might not be in any danger at all.

Roarke stood quietly inside her bedroom door, allowing her time to think. While she appreciated his silence, she wondered if it was a deliberate attempt to frighten her into doing what he wanted.

His presence alone seemed to be wearing her down. An hour ago, before her shower, she'd worried that

Roarke might physically assault her. Now he stood in her bedroom and she had little fear of him. Of course he'd just oh-so-sweetly, oh-so-innocently warned her that she might risk her life unless she did as he asked, and she couldn't help wondering once again if he'd done so deliberately. Was his intention to keep her off balance? Frighten her into leaving her work?

She dropped her hands to her lap, squared her shoulders and lifted her head until their eyes met. Usually she was good at reading people, but he stood so still, so composed, letting his gorgeous face do his persuading for him. And his blue, blue eyes gave away nothing.

"I'm not leaving the country."

"Then we go to plan B."

He surprised her by adapting to her refusal so easily. "Plan B?"

"We find a place to hide here. I'll find someone to keep you safe while I figure out who wants to hurt you. And why."

Alexandra shook her head. "I can't go into hiding." She'd already lost most of the afternoon, a good part of her work day. Her construction schedule demanded that she keep to it or cost overruns would occur. She needed to complete her first building on time, within budget. "I should have gone back to my office this afternoon. But I must be on the job site tomorrow morning at 6:00 a.m. sharp."

Roarke let out a long sigh and glanced at her sideways, no doubt checking to see if she noticed his extraordinary patience with her. "I don't like plan C. It's risky. It means hiding you someplace different every night. It means you wear a bullet-proof vest. It means protecting you—"

"I don't think anyone is after me." Alexandra stood, turned toward her bed and kneeled. She pulled a small suitcase out from under her mattress.

She could feel his eyes drilling into her back searchingly. When she glanced up at him, his plastic expression changed to one of feigned interest in her opinion. "Why?"

"Because as that man chased me through my house, he said he only wanted the stuff my brother sent me."

He shot her a conspiratorial smile as if they shared a joke. "And you believe him?"

"I'm not sure what I believe." She shrugged and unzipped the carry-on bag. She kept travel-size toiletries ready to go, so she just needed to pack a few changes of clothes. "But I don't intend to spend another night here where I can be easily found." She glared at him defiantly. "I'm going to a friend's house."

She tossed the envelope Jake had sent her onto the bed along with clothes, a second pair of shoes and a long T-shirt to sleep in. She expected Roarke to protest. Instead he walked over to her bed; she ignored him. Without a doubt, a man like him didn't get ignored often. He shifted from foot to foot, and she gave him six seconds to try to change her mind.

"You'd be safer if you stayed with me."

He'd lasted two and a half. But she remained silent, knowing if she gave him reasons, he'd argue and wear her down.

When she said nothing, he eyed the envelope with curiosity. "Did that come from your brother?"

She saw no point in denying it when he need merely flip it over and read the return address. "Yes."

"May I look?"

He was sweetly asking her permission? She didn't understand the man. He'd ordered her to take a shower, threatened to do it himself if she didn't, then when she'd boldly said no to his plan A and plan B, he hadn't argued. Much. Hadn't insisted on doing everything his way.

And now he was asking permission to look at her personal papers? He seemed capable of adapting faster than she could take her next breath.

Maybe he would see something important in the papers that she had missed. "Sure, go ahead and take a look. I have no idea what the fuss is all about. Maybe I should just have given the intruder what he wanted."

"That wouldn't have been a good idea."

"Why not? Then he'd leave me alone."

He picked up the envelope. "Jake thinks your mother gave her life to protect this information."

She frowned at his serious expression. Once again he'd surprised her by directing the topic of conversation in a brand-new direction. "My mother?"

"Your biological mother."

"Oh." Alexandra had no memories of the woman who'd given birth to her and thought of her adopted mother as her Mom. Although she'd never been told how her biological mother had died, Roarke spoke as if she'd been involved in some kind of crusade. Alexandra had gone through the pictures and read some of the papers that Jake had sent, but she'd seen no obvious cause that her mother might have been caught up in.

To think that the woman who'd given her birth had felt so passionately about something that she'd risked her own life gave Alexandra a measure of pain and pride. Pain that she and her siblings meant less to her mother than a cause. Pain that the family had been split up. Pride that her mother believed in something so strongly she would risk her life.

Roarke removed the documents and looked at the old black-and-white photographs first. He studied each one for a long time, as if memorizing details before moving on to the next. Eventually he put them aside and perused the birth certificates. Finally, he turned to the pages from her mother's diary.

Alexandra finished packing as he skimmed, wondering if he'd find them more interesting than she had. The pages seemed dull to her, full of chitchat about people she didn't know. None of the material seemed terribly important, nothing controversial or political.

Roarke looked up suddenly but his thoughts seemed far away. He carefully placed all the items back into the envelope and handed them to her. "On the surface, the information seems innocent enough."

"What do you mean by 'on the surface?'"

"The diary pages seem stilted. Either your mother was a poor writer or she might have been using a code. It's also possible that a microdot might be imbedded in the paper."

She looked up sharply. "What?"

"It's a decades-old technique used to send covert information."

How did he know this stuff? Suddenly she wondered just why her brother had picked this man to protect her. What kind of life had he led? Where had he come from?

Obviously, he was well educated. And just as obviously he knew about guns and electronic microphones. She suspected he used that face and body to hide his keen intelligence.

She focused on the new details, thinking hard. "Who would care about old information after so many years? And besides, my brother said these papers are copies."

"Just because they're copies doesn't mean they shouldn't be carefully guarded."

"I don't understand. Why can't we make copies, keep one set, give the other set to the bad guys and hope they leave me alone?"

"Look, suppose the papers include the directions to make some kind of weapon? Would we want our enemies or terrorists to have a copy?"

Weapons? Terrorists? She swallowed hard. "I see what you mean."

"Eventually we may have to take these papers to a friend of mine who is good with codes, but meanwhile, I suggest we make a duplicate set and put them in a very safe place. We have to make sure neither copy falls into the wrong hands."

He'd said *we*, and she wasn't sure if she wanted him to know where she was going to conceal the documents. But then again, if he'd come for the papers, he could have taken them. While his verbal attempts to convince her to trust him had failed, his actions spoke louder. For the first time she really thought he might be telling her the truth. Her brother might indeed have hired him. And that meant her brother really did think she might be in danger.

As she thought over the implications and considered several hiding places, she lifted her packed bag onto the bed and then picked up her phone. "I need to phone my friend and tell her I'm spending the night."

Again he plucked the phone from her fingertips. "Not from here."

Just when she almost believed his story, he did something suspicious. She didn't want to ride in a car with him until she'd told at least one person where she was and who was with her. "Why not from here?"

"Just a precaution. Your phone might be bugged."

Another silver-tongued lie? Or was he really trying to keep her safe? "Why don't you open the receiver and check?"

"Because while there might be a device placed inside your phone, there are several other ways to eavesdrop electronically. A satellite could pick up your call if you use a portable phone like this one. So could a van parked two blocks away. Or a device could be placed in the line connecting your house to the phone company."

He had an answer for everything. Who was this guy? He sounded like a master spy or a very convincing storyteller.

And she had no idea what she should do next. Go along with him and hope he stopped at a pay phone? Or scream bloody murder and hope someone called the police?

ROARKE READ the suspicion in her eyes, beautiful whiskey-colored eyes that reminded him of the changing color of autumn leaves in Virginia. As the golden hues darkened to a vibrant amber, Alexandra's wariness returned with the same steadiness with which winter followed fall.

He should never have accepted a mission over the phone. Roarke knew better. But he'd been eager to show Jake Cochran how good he was. Jake ran a huge P.I. agency that was about to expand nationwide, and Roarke needed steady work.

He should have thought it odd that with all of her brother's connections in the business, Jake had asked Roarke to protect his sister. But Roarke now knew why her brother had chosen him. And it scared him right down to his bones.

Jake must have researched Roarke's background. Through his resources, he might have learned of Roarke's service in the Central Intelligence Agency. He had been a case officer in Bangkok, chief of station in Amsterdam, chief of operations for Africa, and finally chief of counter terrorism.

Did Jake suspect terrorists were after his sister? Had he hired Roarke because he'd once specialized in such things? Roarke should have asked more questions, and now Jake wasn't answering his phone. Another sign that something bigger than Roarke had expected might be happening.

Roarke had quit his job at the CIA to get away from those types of deadly operations. He no longer wanted to live with the indiscriminate killings, with having to send good men and women to their deaths. Roarke had had enough of death. But death might be stalking his client.

However, he saw no reason to share his knowledge

or suspicions with Alexandra. While the woman had a great deal of courage, she disliked him for some reason. He supposed that, under the circumstances, he should have expected some mistrust. But he was frustrated that every time he thought he might be making progress, she withdrew from his friendly overtures. Although obviously intelligent, she didn't seem to believe a word he said.

Puzzling. Roarke had often used his intelligence, his looks and his sex appeal in the world of espionage to coax information out of unsuspecting women for his country's benefit. But Alexandra wasn't most women.

Roarke wondered if she could sense the greatest failure of his life. Could she smell the mess that had soiled a pristine career? Fifty-five people had died in the embassy bombing because of a decision he'd made. But when he closed his eyes, just one face haunted him, that of Sydney, his fiancée, an embassy translator whose dreams had been cut short.

Hours after the disaster, he'd found her in the rubble, and she'd looked as though she were sleeping. No blood. No broken bones or grotesquely bent limbs. No grievous injuries. She'd looked perfect. Only she hadn't been breathing.

The autopsy report said she'd suffered a broken neck. She'd died instantly. He took no comfort in that. She hadn't had time to say goodbye. Hadn't had time to live. She'd been only twenty-five years old.

And he'd blamed himself. For five years he'd had to live with the knowledge that he could have prevented her death. A useless death in an African nation most Americans had never heard of and didn't care about.

Sydney had cared. And she'd paid for her caring with her life. All because of him. Sick at heart, he'd resigned.

Now, he preferred to protect people by risking his own neck. But he hadn't considered that this level of expertise might be needed when he accepted the job of protecting Alexandra. Roarke now sensed something very dangerous about her situation.

To be safe, she should go into hiding—but she'd refused, insisting on attending the inspection of her building and risking her life. Just as Sydney had refused to leave her job at the embassy when the country had erupted into violence.

Roarke wasn't about to lose another woman, especially one entrusted into his care. But maybe he was being over-cautious after his experiences in Africa. Perhaps Alexandra was right. Maybe the intruder had wanted just the package, not her.

His job would be easier if Alexandra trusted him, so he'd make concessions. He would agree to let her go to the inspection for now. He'd let her spend the night with a friend for tonight.

She was scowling at him as she slung her bag over her shoulder. He would have offered to carry it for her, but he needed to keep his hands free. "We're at our most vulnerable point as we leave your apartment. Stay close."

He drew his gun from his holster and placed the weapon in his pocket. Alexandra lagged behind. He turned to see her gazing wistfully at the phone. "Come on. I've a cell phone in my car parked two blocks away." While a normal cell phone was easy to eavesdrop on, his had special modifications. "You can use mine."

She should have been grateful. Instead, the scowl lines on her forehead deepened. He wondered why he longed to rub the scowl lines away. Or to assure her he would keep her safe. He should never have taken a job to protect a woman. Since Sydney's death, he'd roamed the world taking random assignments, rescuing a kidnapped businessman in Colombia, protecting an Arab sheik in Qatar, helping a Jewish family emigrate from Russia. But he'd never guarded a woman. Especially one who reminded him of Sydney.

In looks they were nothing alike. Sydney had had blond hair, hazel eyes and lush curves on her five-foot-two frame. Alexandra was taller, slimmer, delicate despite her height, which he guessed was about five-foot-eight. While she had the most amazing almond-colored eyes with droplets of gold fire, it was her spirit that reminded him of Sydney. Both women cared passionately about their work.

While Sydney had wanted to make the world a better place to live in, Alexandra dreamed of building better places for people to work in. Every time she glanced at her blueprints, her eyes softened and took on a dreamy warmth. He wondered how he'd feel if she ever looked at him like that.

Instead she preferred to give him frowns and scowls of disbelief. If she thought his offer to let her use his cell phone was simply a ruse to get her into his car, she'd find out differently. He hadn't resorted to violence when she'd kicked his shin. He hadn't barged in on her shower. He intended to keep his word to her.

Eventually she would learn that he was a man of honor.

He reached out, took her wrist and tugged her beside him. "When I say close, I mean close."

"Okay. O-kay."

He dropped her wrist before she yanked back, giving her a moment to make up her own mind. Not that she had a choice, and he supposed she knew that and didn't like it, but she adjusted to his demand. Under no circumstances would he compromise her safety.

He hesitated by her front door. While he wanted her to trust him, he knew better. He looked into those magnificent eyes and knew no explanation would suffice. She was as stubborn as two mules. So he resorted to what had worked before—a threat. "When it comes to your safety, I'll do whatever is necessary to keep you alive—even if that means tying your hands behind your back, gagging you, tossing you over my shoulder and carrying you out of here."

Her eyes flashed yellow darts of fire. "You're a Neanderthal!"

"When I say cooperate, it's not to hear myself talk." He made his voice soothing to take away the sting of his words. Peering back down the empty hallway, he hoped she might accept his explanation now that he'd knocked away her complacence. He needed her wary—but not of him. "If someone starts shooting, I want you close enough so I can protect you with my body. Understand?"

Her eyes widened and she swallowed hard. Her fingers tightly clutched the strap of her bag, but for once, she didn't argue.

They walked out of her apartment into the hot, humid air, and his every nerve cell fired on alert. The apartment faced a busy two-lane highway, but after exiting her place, they took a side egress that led to a smaller street and a subdivision of modest houses. He scanned ahead, from side to side, looking for the slightest movement, a shadow that didn't belong, a glint of metal reflecting off a weapon.

''It looks good,'' he murmured softly as they stepped onto a brick sidewalk outside her complex. ''Just another two blocks—''

An ice-cream truck drove by, and Roarke stepped behind a giant magnolia and pulled her with him. Mixing with the scent of magnolia blossoms, he took in the scent of her vanilla shampoo and a floral deodorant. She smelled good. Too good. And he realized that if anyone was hunting them from downwind, they'd smell her in the dark at twenty yards.

He'd have to educate her. He reminded himself once again that she knew nothing about surveillance, terrorism and counterterrorism. She lived in a world where people locked their doors and believed they were safe from prying eyes. She lived in a world where people didn't sleep with a gun under their pillow, another under the mattress and a knife on the nightstand. She lived in a world where she could go to sleep knowing she'd awaken safe in the morning.

Except someone believed she had something valuable in her possession. And they might be willing to kill to get it.

Danger came from an unexpected direction. Not a van of terrorists across the street, but an SUV driven by a harried-looking mother.

As the woman, her SUV filled with noisy kids and

groceries, pulled up to the curb, she waved to Alexandra. And Alexandra's face wore a too-wide smile.

It was the first time he'd seen her grin. A grin that lit up her sparkling topaz eyes and brightened her oval face. He automatically knew she was up to no good.

Damn it! She didn't trust him, and she was about to engage her neighbor in a conversation. Didn't she realize that whoever was after her would return? Ask questions? Just by talking to the woman, Alexandra could be putting her neighbor and her kids in danger.

Without hesitating, Roarke did the first thing he could think of to keep her from calling out a hello. He swung her around, took her into his arms and kissed her full on the mouth.

Her lips parted under his. In surprise?

He meant to pull away as soon as the neighbor drove on by. He meant to pull back and explain why he had to stop her from talking to her neighbor. He meant the kiss to distract her from verbally calling out attention to either of them. But his resolution flew by the wayside the moment his lips touched hers.

She was amazing.

Alexandra fitted against him as if she were made for him. Without awkwardness, without a jostling of hips, noses or elbows. She fitted exactly right. Seemingly of their own accord, his arms drew her closer.

He'd expected her to kick his shin again. Shout a protest. But she didn't pull back. Her arms were around his neck, her fingers in his hair.

And she tasted like savory mints. Smelled like new-mown grass and Florida sunshine. She was making his pulse skip and slide and the blood was rushing up his neck to his brain until he felt dizzy.

Dizzy from wanting her. Dizzy from tasting her.

And she wasn't bony as he'd first thought, but lean and toned and very excitingly feminine.

And she was kissing him back with an enthusiasm that was making his bones melt into a puddle of sizzling need.

God! She was hot.

And he was on fire.

He must have lost his mind. There could be no other possible explanation for how good he felt. Roarke Stone had finally lost it. He was flipping out over a kiss from a woman who didn't even like him.

He had no business messing with a client. He was working a case. Even as he held her close and tasted more of those exciting lips and sipped at her tongue, he could think of a million reasons to stop kissing her.

Except he didn't want to stop. He wanted to let the glorious sensations cascade over him like a waterfall of warm, sexy rain. He wanted to explore her mouth, her chin, her collarbone. Take hours to learn where to touch her to drive her crazy.

What the hell was happening here?

Before his hand moved from her waist, under her shirt, up to discover her breasts, he had to force himself to pull back. It took every ounce of willpower he had to lift his head, to look down into her dazed face, her splendidly passion-shocked eyes and watch her recover.

"Wh-what…? Why? Why did you…?" Completely stunned, she stepped back, her legs unsteady, her expression baffled as she recovered from that amazing kiss.

As her passion slowly dissipated, her former wariness reasserted itself. As she struggled to regroup, he might have laughed to cover his unease, but he hadn't quite recovered either.

Just what the hell had happened here? That amazing kiss. This ripping attraction between them. She had to feel it, too.

And she looked none too happy about it.

Chapter Four

Alexandra staggered back from Roarke's devastating kiss totally baffled. Had that been real hunger in his mesmerizing blue eyes? Or was the man so practiced at kissing that he had the correct expression down pat?

He wasn't just a great kisser, he was in a league all his own. He was an out-of-this-world kisser. The best. The greatest. Unfortunately, he was also arrogant, deceptive and conniving.

And she didn't like him—a fact she'd stupidly forgotten once his lips had touched hers. Her own reactions had betrayed her. Her brain had ceased working. Her heart pumped red-hot blood into her neck and face until she'd felt flushed. Her lungs wouldn't draw enough air. And her legs were weak as a newborn foal's.

He reached for her again, as if knowing exactly how much his lips on hers had affected her. But if he thought one kiss would make her malleable, he'd soon learn otherwise. She had to stay on her guard—especially now that she knew how vulnerable she was to him.

That kiss had come out of nowhere. He'd taken her

totally by surprise, and she regretted not being able to somehow notify her neighbor of her plight. "Whatever possessed you to—"

"Sorry." He apologized easily, but she could see from the light in his eyes that he didn't regret his actions one bit. "I couldn't let you speak to your neighbor."

"Why not?" She folded her arms over her chest, feeling cold despite the heat of the late-afternoon sun.

"Someone might question her later." He eyed her calmly, shooting her his please-be-reasonable look.

"Someone like the police?"

The accusation popped out of Alexandra's mouth before she could stop it. Damn!

Her lapse of judgment had to be due to that stunning kiss. Even now, a minute or so later, her lips still recalled his scorching touch, her body still tingled and her pulse had yet to return to normal. Roarke's face didn't change expression at her slip-up, making her wonder if she'd ever fooled him at all.

He explained patiently. "The intruder who broke the chain on your front door used force. You want to take a chance he might apply the same technique on your neighbor?"

A single mom with three kids? She wouldn't have risked it if she'd known her actions could place the woman in danger, although there was no guarantee the man still might not question her neighbor. Alexandra swallowed hard, understanding that he'd assessed the situation and acted before she'd even considered the possibilities. Or was he feeding her another line to keep anyone from knowing that she was with him?

"I didn't think—"

"It's okay. That's why I'm here." He held out his hand to her. "It would make my job easier if you'd at least give me the benefit of the doubt."

Recalling how fast he could move, she knew she couldn't possibly escape him if she learned he really wasn't trustworthy. After clearly showing him how little she trusted him, she tried to repair the damage by putting her hand in his.

His hand closed around hers lightly, but it might as well have been a stainless-steel handcuff. He held her trapped and it made her heartbeat quicken again. She'd feel much better about her situation once he let her use his cell phone.

They walked the next block to a white sedan parked beneath a towering oak. She memorized the license plate and, as he unlocked the door, she searched for the phone he'd promised to lend her.

Roarke opened the door for her, and she verified that the door handles were still there in case she wanted to make a quick exit. They were. But she still hesitated. Knowing the locks were placed by the driver's hand, she remained extremely reluctant to get inside. Especially when she saw no sign of a phone.

"Where's your phone?"

Roarke leaned inside and ran his hand in the crack between the seat and the backrest. "My car's in the shop. This is a rental. I must have left my phone in the other car this morning."

"How convenient."

She stepped back, and Roarke straightened. "Not for me. Not if the mechanic runs up my bill. We can stop at a pay phone," he offered when instead of moving toward the passenger seat she retreated another step.

She had known he'd have another perfectly logical explanation, but her suspicions went on overdrive. This time she made no pretense of hiding them. "You wouldn't let me call the cops from my apartment. You wouldn't let me talk to my neighbor. And now I can't use your cell phone. Not one person in this world knows I'm with you." She snapped her fingers. "I could disappear and you could get away with—"

"Murder?" He leaned back and rested his hands on his narrow hips. "If I wanted to kill you, you wouldn't have made it off your back terrace. Or out of the Dumpster."

She thought of that raging-hot kiss. "Maybe murder isn't what you had in mind."

"Now you think I'm a rapist?"

It sounded ridiculous when he put it like that. She realized if rape had been his intention, he could have overpowered her back in her apartment.

"I don't know what or who you are."

"I told you—"

"And why should I believe you? Because you beat up that man in my apartment?"

"You didn't protest at the time," he countered.

"You're deliberately missing the point. You carry a gun."

"I have a permit."

"Which I'm sure isn't on you, right? You talk about terrorists as casually as other men talk about football. And I have no idea why you expect me to believe a word you say." She didn't even pause for breath.

"And you've given me no proof that my brother hired you."

"Actually, I have no proof until Jake returns, and he isn't answering his calls."

"I suppose Jake didn't pay you by check?"

"He had his assistant Harrison wire cash."

"Then we could talk to him," she suggested.

"You can try. I've called several times and he's always out."

Alexandra rolled her eyes. "Oh, this just keeps getting better and better."

Roarke didn't flex one muscle. "Exactly what would you like me to do?"

She gestured with her hand. "Go away. You're fired."

Roarke shook his head. "You can't fire me because you didn't hire me."

So exactly how was she going to get rid of him? She didn't get into cars with strangers.

"How about a compromise?" he offered.

"I'm listening."

"I'll walk you back to your car. You drive me back here. I'll follow you to your friend's house and make sure you're okay."

"You'd do that?"

"Yes."

"You won't insist on coming inside?"

"No."

Under his plan, she'd still have to get into a vehicle with him, but she would be driving. But he still had his gun. He could force her to drive anywhere he wanted her to go.

He must have seen the refusal in her eyes. Before

she could let out a scream, he picked her up and dumped her into the front seat of his car, then leaned over and snapped on her seat belt.

Hands trembling, she fumbled for the release. Just when he'd about convinced her he was looking out for her safety, he'd used force against her. She might not be hurt, but she didn't trust him. Maybe he was one of those sickos who captured women and kept them for years in a basement.

Maybe he intended to kidnap her for ransom. Her parents would pay well for her safe return.

He vaulted across the hood. She had to get away. The seat belt clicked open and retracted. She reached for the door handle.

He slid into the driver's seat. And then he shot her one of those charming grins. "It's going to be okay. Tell me where your friend lives."

She knew better than to believe him. Fear made her sweat on the outside, but she felt as if she'd swallowed a snowball and her insides froze.

Frantic, Alexandra yanked on the door.

Calmly, Roarke reached across her and shut the door, the loud slam one of sickening finality that sealed her fate. He had her trapped, had her just where he wanted her.

She tried to bite his arm, claw his face, elbow him in the neck. She missed. Opened her mouth to scream.

"Don't yell. I won't hurt you."

"Then prove it," she demanded.

"How?"

"Give me your gun," she suggested.

Without hesitation, Roarke pulled out his gun, and

sheer terror paralyzed her. She shouldn't have re-minded him of the weapon.

Then he handed her the gun—butt first.

What the hell? She'd thought he was going to shoot her. Thought these breaths were her last.

"Here. Take it."

She accepted the weapon. Heavier than she would have imagined, it fit her hand and restored some of her confidence. She knew a little about guns. Her father had taught her how to shoot when she was a kid. The safety was on, which meant if she pulled the trigger the weapon wouldn't fire.

She released the clip at the bottom, checked to make sure the weapon had bullets and then snapped the clip back into place. Without hesitation she flipped off the safety, but she didn't point the weapon at Roarke. The first two things her dad had drummed into her were to treat every gun as if it was loaded and never to point the weapon at anything unless she wanted to shoot at it. And all of a sudden, she wasn't so sure she could shoot Roarke Stone.

"Feel safer now?" He looked as cool as a talk-show host in front of a nationwide audience, not the least perturbed that she'd accepted his weapon and might decide to shoot him.

She couldn't believe that her voice sounded almost normal. "I'd feel better if you didn't have a backup gun in your—"

"Ankle holster." He sent her a you-wouldn't-dare-shoot-me grin and started the engine.

Hot air blasted from the air conditioner, and he rolled down the windows a few inches to release the heat. He snapped off the radio and retrieved a pair of dark sunglasses from beneath the sun visor.

"Why did you give me this gun?"

"You looked scared."

She scowled at him. "I am scared."

"I won't hurt you."

Easy for him to say. Easier for her to believe now that she had his weapon. She suspected he might be able to knock the gun from her hand before she could pull the trigger, but simply holding the weapon had lessened her panic. That he'd given it to her revealed that he understood her fear and wanted to ease it.

At least she now knew he wasn't one of those wackos who fed off women's anxieties to make themselves feel more powerful. But maybe he simply enjoyed toying with her. Maybe the bullets were blanks.

She didn't think so. "Turn right at the corner and take Beach Boulevard west."

Roarke followed her directions, and, as the hot air cooled, her breathing started to return to normal. Beside her, Roarke drove smoothly, but she noted how every few seconds he checked the rearview mirror.

"Is anything wrong?" She wondered if she'd been worried about the wrong thing. While she still didn't trust Roarke, perhaps she'd overlooked an even larger threat.

"I'm not sure. We may have picked up a tail." He gave her the bad news as if he was reporting the weather. Nothing in his demeanor changed. Not his posture, his expression or his tone of voice. Did the man have nerves of steel?

She started to turn around to look for their tail.

"Use the side-view mirror. Watch, I'm going to change lanes. See if that silver sedan does, too."

Sure enough, when Roarke switched lanes, the other car followed, but remained three cars back. He glanced over at her and the gun she still held. "You might want to put the safety back on and refasten your seat belt."

"You need to drive faster?"

He nodded. "You aren't going to shoot me for not following your directions while I try and lose this guy, are you?"

Without comment, she did as he asked. But she kept the weapon firmly in hand as Roarke swung a quick right, a left, another left and then pulled behind a building and into someone's private covered parking area.

"I don't know if the men chasing us have access to satellite surveillance but if they do, the roof should prevent an eye in the sky from spotting us."

"A satellite can pick out a car?" she asked, appreciating that once again his knowledge might have saved her.

"Those birds can read a license plate. But it's difficult to get priority usage. I'm hoping we aren't that high up on the food chain to warrant that kind of a close look."

She saw the silver sedan drive by and realized she'd been holding her breath. Slowly, she forced herself to let it go. If not for Roarke's quick thinking, those men would have caught them. Caught her.

Still frightened, but trusting Roarke more every minute, she leaned back and wondered what she'd do if she were alone. Drive straight to the police station? Call her folks, who were out of town, for help?

Twenty minutes later, Roarke stopped at a convenience store and she called her friend at work. Her friend wasn't coming home tonight and offered Alexandra her house at the beach. Glad that Bonnie wouldn't be there since she no longer wanted to chance putting any of her friends in danger, she memorized where Bonnie kept the key. Third flower pot to the right of the front door.

At her friend's beachfront home, Alexandra could relax. She hoped the ocean-view room with a terrace and the soothing sounds of the waves lapping on Jacksonville's white sand would restore her nerves.

Alexandra returned to Roarke without fear. "All set. Bonnie's spending the night with her boyfriend."

"You're not afraid to be alone?"

"Why should I be? No one will know where I am."

And she could work. Make up for the lost hours this afternoon. She had to get her mind back on business. Tomorrow the second-story concrete would be poured on her building. City inspectors would check to ensure quality control, and she didn't want anything to go wrong.

As she glanced at the man driving the car, she needed to figure out what to do. After spending an afternoon with him, she believed her brother really had hired Roarke Stone to protect her. But she intended to check on Roarke's credentials and speak with her brother to see if he had any idea why anyone would be after the papers he'd sent.

When Roarke pulled up to the beach house, she still held the gun tightly gripped in her hand. He shut off the car's engine. "You can keep the gun tonight, but I suggest you keep it out of sight."

"Thanks."

"For what?"

She held up the weapon. "For this." She'd never understood why women didn't like guns. Sure they were noisy. And they were only as good as the person using them. But they were a tool that equalized the sexes. And she felt safer for having the weapon, safer because she knew how to use it.

Jake's ruse to avoid the tail worked and she was grateful that her brother had sent a bodyguard who understood the enemy's modus operandi. The tiny house with its steeply pitched roof and hurricane shutters sat back from the road among sand dunes planted with sea oats. While the yard butted almost right up to neighbors on either side, Alexandra knew from having stayed there often as a guest that the magnificent oceanfront view and powdery white sand beach gave visitors a feeling of endless vistas and privacy.

Jake walked beside her up the white-brick sidewalk. Several women sunbathing on a neighbor's porch gave Jake's perfect good looks second glances. Stares.

He noticed, but it didn't deter him from politely holding the flowerpot for her while she retrieved the key. Nor did it keep him from scanning the tiled hallway as she unlocked the door.

He motioned her back. "Wait here."

Two minutes later he returned. "It's clear. You sure you don't want me to spend the night?"

"Very sure."

Let him spend the night? No way. She wouldn't get a lick of work done. She wouldn't be able to check out his credentials. And no way would she sleep a wink if he remained under the same roof. Besides, the bungalow only had one bedroom and Roarke wouldn't fit on the couch.

He lifted the sunglasses up from his nose onto his forehead. Blue eyes searched hers, shooting slivers of heat to her core. "You aren't frightened?"

Right now her primary fear was her reaction to this man. She didn't like her inability to stop noticing how good he looked. She didn't want to think about him— especially when she really, really didn't like him— especially when she recalled that sizzling kiss that had fused her brain cells and that definitely shouldn't ever have happened.

She escorted him to the door and firmly led him over the threshold. "No one knows I'm here. I'll be fine."

He stopped and looked at her. "Lock this door behind me and don't open it for anyone. Don't go anywhere."

"Like I have a car."

Her response, automatically flippant, concealed her amazement. She may have kissed the man, but she really didn't know him. Yet, for the first time she realized that his concern for her was genuine. He didn't want to leave her alone in case she needed his protection. There was more to him than a pretty face, a big strong bod and a working brain. He cared, and she hated the fact that she liked knowing he cared.

"You won't need your car. I'll pick you up tomorrow morning at…?"

"Five."

And by then she'd have her galloping emotions

back under control. She'd have sorted out the danger. And she'd have arranged for another bodyguard to replace Roarke Stone.

THREE HOURS LATER she settled on the sofa with a glass of chardonnay, more perplexed than ever. She hadn't been able to contact her brother Jake and couldn't bring herself to leave the first message between them since they were children on an impersonal voice mail. She reminded herself to try again in the morning.

Next, she'd verified Roarke's credentials, and Alexandra was no longer sure she should replace him. She'd called a reporter friend she'd known in high school and Linda had done a quick computer search on Roarke Stone.

He was ex-CIA! Apparently very highly thought of. He'd been the youngest station chief and then had operated a specialized counter-terrorism group. There was no mention of a wife or family. And he'd been investigated and cleared after some trouble with an African embassy. Roarke had quit shortly after the incident and dropped out of the news.

His bodyguard service was relatively new. So new he didn't have a listing in this year's phone book. She dialed information and an operator confirmed a new listing.

Feeling a little more secure after verifying that Roarke's business at least had an address and a phone number, Alexandra moved onto the back deck. The sun went down over the land behind her, shooting a marvelous sparkle of burnished orange and yellow light across the ocean. Overhead, gulls cawed and dived into the sea for food. A light breeze carried the salty ocean tang, and she allowed the tensions of the day to evaporate in the cooling air.

Although she'd learned new facts about Roarke, they'd confirmed her earlier impressions. He was smart, determined and skilled at what he did. Briefly, she wondered why he'd quit his job with the CIA after his spectacular rise to a very high position. Clearly he'd once been ambitious. Yet she hadn't sensed that in him at all, and she found it strange.

She stared at the Atlantic and finished the glass of wine, suspecting she couldn't have a better man than Roarke Stone to protect her. She might not like the way she responded to Roarke, but Jake had chosen wisely. But why hadn't her brother called her? Explained what was going on? How could she make informed decisions with so little information?

Later, she would read her mother's diary more carefully. Maybe she'd find answers there. But where would she find answers to her heart-stopping reaction to Roarke's kiss? Never had she responded to a man as she had to him.

She could tell herself it was her fear, the unaccustomed life-and-death situation that made her heart kick her ribs and her blood rush from her head. But that kiss was indelibly imprinted on her brain, and she could recall the most subtle details of her embarrassingly passionate response to a stranger that she didn't even particularly like.

Even after the danger had passed, her heart had skipped a little every time he'd looked at her with those piercing blue eyes. She was aware of every nuance of his expression, of a slight upward rise of his

lip, of the arch of his brow, of the light of amusement
in his eyes when he teased her into doing what he
wanted.

She knew better than to blame her heightened fears
on her reaction to Roarke. If he came up behind her
now and kissed her neck, shivers would shimmy down
to her core. Was it lust? He was a damn good-looking
man. But if Mel Gibson or Brad Pitt showed up on
Bonnie's patio, would she notice every little thing
about them as she did with Roarke? Would she be so
intensely aware of their masculinity that she forgot
where she was and that she might be in danger?

She didn't think so. Somehow Roarke had wormed
his way under her defenses, and she didn't like it one
damn bit. She didn't need any complications in her
life right now. She had her skyscraper to build and a
thousand details to take care of.

Turning away from the ocean, she returned to the
bungalow and worked for several hours. She ate a
bowl of cereal for dinner and an apple for dessert before crawling into bed exhausted. She expected to
close her eyes and immediately fall asleep.

But every time she closed her eyes, Roarke appeared. His face peering into the Dumpster at her in
amusement. His real annoyance and genuine respect
when she'd defied him and tried to escape out the
bathroom window. His reluctance to leave her alone
for the night.

Tossing onto her side, she punched the pillow, wishing it was his face. The man had disturbed her waking
hours, must he disturb her sleep, too?

She flicked on the television and changed the channels without finding anything to hold her interest.

Restless, tired, she wanted to take a long walk on the beach. But until she knew who was after her and why, she'd remain safe behind locked doors. Although she didn't think anyone could find her here, she wouldn't take foolish risks with her life.

She had too much to live for.

Eventually, in the wee hours of the morning, she fell asleep and it seemed as though only minutes passed before her alarm buzzed her awake. Cranky before her morning coffee, she quickly took a shower and dressed, refusing to fuss over the circles under her eyes. Maybe if she didn't look good, Roarke wouldn't be tempted to...

She glanced out the window and her pulse sped up. A sleek black sports car that hadn't been there last night sat across the street from the bungalow. She could tell from the fogged windows that someone sat inside it. Although it was too far away to identify the driver or read the license plates, she wondered if he was the same man who'd crashed into her apartment. Had he found her again? Or was he simply an innocent stranger carpooling with a neighbor? She had a half hour until she expected Roarke, but she refused to panic. Maybe the guy had just stopped to answer a call of nature. Or read a map. Or eat breakfast. Maybe he wanted to watch the sun come up over the ocean.

But he could be the same man who'd chased her through her apartment. The one who wanted the package her brother had sent.

Better not to take any chances.

Alexandra picked up the phone and called the police.

Chapter Five

"Please, hurry. Someone's at the back door." Alexandra hung up the phone and rushed to the nightstand and the gun Roarke had left her. She slipped off the safety and backed against the wall, holding her breath.

Listening hard.

Someone was here, possibly already inside the bungalow.

She didn't hear footsteps so much as sense the presence of another person. Suddenly she wished she hadn't sent Roarke away last night. She'd been so certain she was safe. And now she was alone.

Thank God he'd left her a gun. Gripping the weapon firmly, she peered out into the darkness. But she saw no movement except the waves lapping against the beach and clouds scudding past a crescent moon.

But the hair on the back of her neck rose, responding to danger she couldn't see.

The police are on the way, she reminded herself. But how long would they take to arrive?

Waiting inside, where an intruder expected her to be, seemed like a stupid move. She backed out the bedroom door onto the wrap-around terrace.

But where should she go? She didn't even have her car since Roarke had driven her here. The beach would provide no cover and the sunrise couldn't be far away.

Deciding that the best place to hide would be in the thick viburnum hedge that ran along the property's side yard, she dropped and rolled off the deck. As soon as she struck the sand, a hand clamped over her mouth, deadening her scream. Arms grabbed her tightly, and she froze as cold fear slithered down her throat and coiled around her heart.

"It's Roarke." His warm whisper in her ear chased away the fear.

But she didn't have time to enjoy her relief before anger overrode all other feelings. A white-hot rage rose up inside her for his frightening her like that.

"Why the hell can't you ring the bell? Or knock? And come through the door like a normal person?" she demanded in a fierce whisper that chased away the last vestiges of fear.

Roarke pulled her under the decking, his strong arms and chest protecting her face from the sand and weeds, his warm breath comforting in her ear. "And take a chance of your shooting me?"

"Very funny. Making jokes while someone's in the house stalking me."

"Not likely."

"What do you mean, not likely?"

"I set up a perimeter alarm. The only one who broke the laser beam was me after you called the police."

Perimeter alarm? Laser beam? "Could you say that in English, not spy talk, please?"

"Last night I took a few precautionary measures. I told you I'd keep you safe."

"No one's in the house?"

"No."

"Then why are we under my deck whispering?"

"I don't want the police to shoot me by mistake. We needed a safe place to talk."

"What's wrong with the living room?" She sighed. "I just don't understand you."

"The living room is where the cops would expect us to be. Some hotshot with a happy trigger finger might decide I'm one of the bad guys," he told her in that sexy whisper that annoyed her much more than she wanted to admit.

She should have known he wouldn't have abandoned her. He took his job too seriously. It would have been much more comfortable for him to have insisted on staying inside the bungalow with her last night. But he hadn't insisted.

Why? Surely it wasn't to make her feel better? Sometimes Roarke could be considerate, but only when it suited his needs. He must have wanted to stay apart from her for a reason. Or he had work to do— work he didn't trust her to know about. The knowledge stung, but she shoved it away.

As if sensing her upset, he sought to calm her. "Did you think I would leave you alone and unprotected?"

She refused to soften at his indignant tone. "Are you saying you've been outside the bungalow all night just so you could spy on me?"

"Yes."

Where was his silver tongue when she needed explanations? ''Then you saw the black Mercedes M420 across the street?''

''That's *my* vehicle,'' he admitted wryly. ''Remember, the other was a loaner?''

''But—''

''A friend dropped it off.''

''But—''

''I never left you for a minute.''

''But, I called the police on you.''

''I know.'' He chuckled that warm, masculine chuckle that irritated her soul.

''How do you know?''

Sirens in the distance warned of approaching police cars. ''I bugged your phone during my search yesterday.''

''Creep.'' He'd not only been spying on her, he'd been listening to her phone calls. Thank God she hadn't called a girlfriend and spoken about him.

''The police are going to show any minute and you'll have to tell them you made a mistake.''

''Pervert.''

''You'll have to explain that you didn't recognize my car and you got scared.''

''And why shouldn't I just let them haul you off or shoot you?''

Roarke grunted as she dug her elbow into his side as she tried to roll away. But he held her close, close enough for her to smell the coffee on his breath. ''You know who I am now. You checked me out with your reporter friend. You know I run a legitimate business, you checked with information. What you also don't know is that last night I got hold of Harrison.''

''Harrison?''

"Your brother's assistant. He told me that Jake is on the run. Harrison will call and let us know as soon as he hears from him."

New fears sprinted through her brain. Although he'd told her that he'd bugged her phone, she still hadn't absorbed all the implications of his confession. Now, with her brother on the run, she couldn't confirm anything Roarke told her. As much as she wanted to pretend none of this was happening, she'd always faced her problems head-on. But she feared if she learned more about what it was like to live in his world, she'd become like Roarke, a man who seemed unable to trust anyone, not a partner, not the local authorities, not even her.

"The less you tell the cops, the faster you'll get to work—assuming you still insist on being there today?"

"It's imperative."

"You did say you needed to be there by six?"

Damn him! "Do you ever *not* get your way?"

Taking her question for agreement, he let her scoot out from beneath the deck. She brushed off the sand, expecting Roarke to follow her and explain the mistake to the police.

But he stayed hidden. And then a flashlight caught her in its beam. "Place your hands above your head. Slowly," a cop ordered.

Alexandra did as she was told, wondering why it was she who'd ended up explaining to the police when it should have been Roarke. He was the one who'd made her nervous by spying on her. He was the one who'd bugged her phone and set up perimeter defenses. His suspicious actions had caused her to call for help. And yet now, when she could use his expertise, he'd suddenly vanished.

Just like Patrick—Roarke was nowhere to be found when she needed him. But since when did she need a man? Especially one like Roarke Stone? She didn't like his methods. Didn't like the way he refused to explain his intentions to her. He'd treated her like a child, and she fully intended to tell him that in the future, they needed to work as a team. He needed to inform her how and where he intended to protect her so she could make intelligent decisions.

This morning had been a fiasco. While she'd avoided telling the police about the man at her apartment yesterday, it still took too long to fill out the paperwork and give her statement about this morning's call.

To top it all off, by the time she finished with the police, she was close to an hour late to the job site. And Roarke had insisted that she pack all her things. He didn't want her to spend another night at the same place, claiming it was too easy for a good hacker to do a computer search on the police records and find her address. She'd stuffed the papers Jake had sent into a briefcase and her clothes into her soft-sided bag. Another fifteen minutes went by before they could drive to her work site.

She showed her pass to the guard at the gate and instructed Roarke to park along the fence. Ignoring the dust in the air, she hurried to inspect the building's northeast section. Her chief engineer was overseeing the cement trucks dumping wet concrete into pump trucks which transported it by hose three hundred feet into wooden forms with a smooth regularity she found comforting. Workers manned vibrating tubes to remove the air from the concrete. At the top of the forms, men checked final placement of rebar as it poked through the concrete.

However, as they strode toward her crew, Alexandra carrying her briefcase, Roarke's next suggestion threw her totally off balance. "Introduce me as your new friend."

She halted in her tracks, grateful for the loud machines which gave them a measure of privacy. "Friend?"

His expression didn't change. His gorgeous face looked as calm as if he were discussing whether to turn right or left. "Boyfriend. Lover. Whatever."

Long after he left, she would have to deal with the consequences of this decision. Introducing him like that to coworkers would have the same effect as if one of her foremen brought a Playboy bunny on site. Roarke's good looks were simply too stunning to avoid speculation. And she wanted the crew's minds on their work.

She scowled at Roarke. "Why can't you be a business associate?"

Her annoyance ricocheted right off him. His eyes lit with amusement at her suggestion, but he scanned the building site with an efficiency that told her not once had he neglected the primary reason for his presence, to protect her. While his presence made her feel safer, she didn't want to think about Roarke when she had work to supervise. Today's concrete pour was the beginning of the culmination of a dream that had begun when she was in high school. She wanted to enjoy the moment. And she didn't want to think about her co-workers' reactions to Roarke's presence.

Even as he raised his voice to be heard above the heavy concrete trucks, he managed to portray an intimacy between them. "Have you forgotten I intend to stick close to you? Real close." His words evoked images of him holding her in his arms, kissing her again. Going further. She fought down a shiver of excitement mixed with fear as he kept speaking. "You're vulnerable here on the construction site."

"We have a guarded gate."

"That guard didn't examine your pass very closely."

"He knows me."

"He didn't ask about me. Suppose I had a gun on you and forced you inside. He wouldn't have known."

"He's a construction security guard. He doesn't work for the FBI."

"Exactly." It irritated her that he thought her words proved the point he'd been trying to make. Once again she wondered what it did to a person always to live with suspicion. But Roarke didn't give her time to speculate. "And we didn't have time to fit you with a bullet-proof vest, copy those papers Jake sent you or hide the originals."

"They should be safe in my briefcase for now, and the construction office has a copy machine. We can make duplicates later. Or you could do it while I work."

He shook his head with a grin—a grin that seemed both persuasive and firm. "My job is to protect you—not necessarily the papers Jake sent."

"Fine."

"I may have to act as your personal body armor, and I can't do that if you're more than two feet from me." His eyes twinkled with an easy confidence that she wanted to slap off his face. "Besides, if you introduce me as your lover, no one will ask questions about the case we don't want to answer."

Instead they'd just speculate endlessly behind her back. And she'd worked too hard in a field dominated by men to win the respect of her employees and associates to allow them to wonder if she might not have her mind on the job because she had a new lover in her life.

As her chief foreman headed over, speculation in his eyes, she had to think fast. She didn't want anyone believing that she'd bring a lover to work with her. She couldn't think of anything more unprofessional. But she understood that Roarke needed a reason to stay close to her.

Think!

Ha! She came up with just the thing.

She knew she should discuss her plan with Roarke, but there wasn't time. Her chief engineer and head foreman tipped their hard hats to her and waited for introductions.

"Sorry I got held up," Alexandra explained. "I'd like you both to meet my brother, Jake Cochran. We were split up when we were adopted and haven't seen one another since. We just reunited. Jake, this is Aaron Blake, my engineer, and our foreman, Tyson Coldwell." As she lied about Roarke's identity, the men shook hands. Not even by the quiver of one inch-long eyelash did Roarke reveal his surprise at her lie. Man, oh, man, he was smooth.

But for once she had him where she wanted him—
at an emotional distance. As her pretend brother, he
couldn't suddenly kiss her to shut her up. He couldn't
take her into his arms, touch her as a lover would.

Her cover story would force him to keep his movements fraternal, and therefore she could keep her mind
on work, where it belonged. She didn't need the dis-
tractions of his searing looks and her undependable
hormones.

Besides, she enjoyed outthinking Roarke. The man
was simply too accustomed to having his own way.
Let him see how it felt to be left out of the loop, and
maybe he'd learn to communicate his own plans a
little better.

But right now, her concern turned to the city building inspectors who checked everything from the concrete's PSI—pounds per square inch—to her paperwork. While she supposed the inspectors were a
necessary evil, they seemed to take pleasure in making
her work more difficult.

The building inspector frowned at her, then looked
at the sky. "You've been lucky we're having a
drought. But if it starts to rain, you'll need heavy plastic ready to cover the pour."

Duh!

Alexandra nodded sweetly through gritted teeth.
While the inspectors needed to justify their cushy jobs,
they wouldn't have done it by pointing out the obvious
to a man, but she'd long ago learned to deal with their
chauvinism.

She turned up her smile a notch. "Thanks for the
reminder. We have several pallets of plastic stored in
a semi-truck. Want to take a look?"

"Won't be necessary." The inspector looked at his watch then at the sky that only had a few high cirrus clouds in sight.

It hadn't rained in months. The state was in the middle of the worst drought in a decade. On the radio Alexandra had heard about fires breaking out in the state parks. And while the dry conditions hurt agriculture and kept the state's fire fighters on full alert, it was perfect weather for pouring concrete.

She supervised work all morning and was pleasantly surprised by how smoothly Roarke synchronized his movements to hers. He could work unobtrusively when he wanted to, and she appreciated his silent efficiency as she dealt with a multitude of minor problems. It was amazing that such a gorgeous man could make himself almost invisible. Somehow he turned down that megawatt smile and the sex appeal, yet she never lost her constant awareness of his presence.

As she worked, she worried over her responsibility to the project. Suppose the intruder interfered with her life again? Suppose she couldn't check on her building with the regularity she preferred? While no one was indispensable and she had a great crew, it still would make sense to warn her coworkers that they might have to pick up the slack if she couldn't supervise on a regular basis.

And yet she hesitated. Roarke had warned her that anyone she confided in might be placed in danger. Personally, she thought he might be way too cautious—but she wouldn't risk other people's lives by telling them the truth.

However, there was no reason she, too, couldn't come up with a plausible story. So, as she worked on the site, she came up with another plan. Just as they broke for lunch, she called over Aaron and Tyson. "I may take off some time here and there to spend with my brother." She tried to look at Roarke with sisterly fondness and absolutely no hint of lust. "We have a lot of catching up to do." Her glance went back to her coworkers. "If I'm out of touch, I hope I can depend on you two to cover for me."

"No problem."

"Count on us."

As her men left, Roarke spoke teasingly in her ear. "Smart thinking. I might make a competent spook out of you yet."

Just like switching up the volume on a CD, he upped his masculine intensity. He stood closer. His mesmerizing eyes appeared bluer, and he almost knocked her over with one of those killer smiles.

All morning she'd worked, and the simmering tension between them had stayed in the background. Suddenly they were alone. And whammo! He radiated enough sex appeal to dance and strip with the Chippendales.

Just the intimacy of his look sucked the moisture from her mouth. She licked her bottom lip, nervously reminding herself that she didn't like Roarke Stone. But she didn't have to like him to allow him to do his job. Nor did she have to respond to the magnetism he projected. Having a man protect her might be inherently sexy, but all she had to do to cool her hormones was remember he'd probably flashed those sexy smiles to a myriad of women.

Grateful for the sunglasses that prevented him from seeing her eyes and hoping he'd think the flush rising up her neck was due to the noonday sun, she told herself to get a grip. Most of the construction people had left, but some had stayed behind to stir and smooth the wet cement.

Although food was the last thing on her mind, she'd like a break from the heat. A cool drink, air-conditioning and people around them were just the ticket to break the spell of intimacy he'd effortlessly woven around them.

She set down her briefcase, removed her hard hat and wiped her brow. "How about lun—?"

Without warning, Roarke tackled Alexandra.

The dusty ground flew up before she could put her hands out to brace herself. The packed earth knocked the air out of her.

Roarke's six-foot-four body fell on top of her.

Her lungs fought to draw air. Couldn't.

Through dizziness, she heard curses. Men climbing down from the scaffolding. Machines stopping.

Roarke sat up and rolled her over, cradling her head in his lap. He leaned and blocked the sun, his irises dark with concern. Gently, his hands smoothed her forehead. "Are you all right?"

Again she tried for a ragged gasp, sounded as if she was choking, still not breathing. Roarke finally got the idea that she couldn't draw air into her burning lungs.

"You got the wind knocked out of you. Try to relax. Give your diaphragm a second to recover."

She was lightheaded; his words came to her from a great distance. He was talking. She knew because she could see his lips moving, but she couldn't hear his words. Couldn't hear the crews or the machines or the nearby traffic.

What the hell happened?

Oh, God. She couldn't breathe.

She was going to suffocate out here on the ground. Blackness closed in.

Alexandra opened her eyes, and the first thing she saw was the face of an angel. He just needed wings and a halo to complete his perfection. With a wet cloth, the prettiest man in the world was wiping her forehead.

Men aren't pretty, she thought groggily.

"Welcome back," the gorgeous hunk told her with a sexy smile, and suddenly everything came back. He wasn't an angel, but Roarke Stone, her bodyguard. Here to protect her.

Instead he'd tried to squash her. No, that couldn't be right.

She raised her head and sipped the water he offered, noting her familiar surroundings. Her briefcase on the floor. A battered desk, fluorescent lights and a fax machine and computer. Someone had carried her from the work site to the construction trailer.

The air-conditioning felt wonderful, but Roarke's gentle hands bathing her forehead with a damp towel were glorious. For a minute she rested, enjoying the contrast between his fierce look of concern and the gentle ministrations of his hands, the coolness of the damp cloth and the warmth of his fingertips.

She shouldn't be enjoying him like this. She tried to sit up and he eased her back onto the couch.

"Take a moment."

"What happened?" Her mouth seemed as dry as old cement and she reached for the water glass with shaking hands.

Roarke beat her to it, lifting her head, holding the glass to her lips. She drank greedily, enjoying the wet coolness as it trickled down her parched throat.

"Easy."

She raised her eyes to look at him. "The last thing I remember was you tackling me."

"I knocked the wind out of your lungs. Sorry. I didn't realize you were so delicate."

"I'm not delicate. You're a brute!"

"I did what was necessary to save your life."

"Huh?" Save her life? She didn't recall any attack, just Roarke knocking her off her feet with the expertise of a pro wrestler. "Was someone shooting at me?"

"Do you remember setting down your briefcase and taking off your hard hat to wipe the perspiration from your forehead?"

"Vaguely"

"I knocked you out of the way when a wrench hurtled down off the scaffolding."

She frowned. "But the crew had knocked off for lunch."

"Exactly. I sent one of the security guards to look around, but they didn't find anything suspicious."

She knew that look of his. Suspicion darkening his blue irises until they appeared dark navy. His lips tightening and a muscle in his neck flickering. He believed someone had deliberately dropped that wrench. "It could have been an accident. Construction sites are notoriously dangerous places. That's why our insurance rates are so high."

"And it's just a coincidence that the wrench fell on you—just after you removed your hard hat? If you believe that, there's a tropical island in the middle of the Arctic Ocean I'd like to sell you.''

She forced herself to a sitting position and warily peered out the window. Her mind wasn't on the construction, the concrete or the building she wanted to create. Someone may have just tried to kill her. If that wrench had landed on her head, her skull would have been squashed like a rotten melon. ''But what's the point of trying to hurt me? We thought this was connected to the materials Jake sent. Dropping a wrench on my head won't give them what they are after.''

Grimly, Roarke crossed his arms over his chest and peered out the dusty trailer window. ''We don't know what they're after. But we need to get you out of here. And it's not going to be easy.''

Chapter Six

Roarke didn't want to worry Alexandra any more than necessary, but he had to make her understand that the danger could come from several directions. Yet he couldn't force himself into scaring her further. Not while her whiskey-gold irises remained dilated from shock. Not while her slender fingers still shook. Not when her normal olive color still hadn't returned to her too-pale cheeks. Although he could have kicked himself for downing her like a sack of potatoes, he'd reacted instinctively to danger, pushing her way too hard to safety, accidentally knocking the wind out of her in his hurry to protect her in case additional tools hurtled down. Although he'd saved her from a terrible injury, his own actions could have hurt her. She'd been lucky he hadn't caused more damage.

It wasn't like him to overreact, but when a tiny metal rattling sound from overhead had caused him to glance up and see that shiny object plummeting down, he'd acted instantly and on pure instinct. And he'd almost done serious harm.

Had his adrenaline surged more strongly since it had been Alexandra in danger? Without a doubt. He couldn't help admiring the woman. She had a good head on her shoulders, plenty of ambition, the drive to accomplish her goals and the courage to see things through. And she had eyes potent enough to make a man tipsy.

Alexandra set down her water glass and brushed some loose sand from the wisps of hair escaping her braid and curling softly around her face. "Don't you think you might be overdoing it?"

She just didn't understand that his world operated by different rules. She was a bright, savvy woman, and he had to keep in mind that life-and-death situations were new to her. But to him, the signs were as clear as the Remember Your Hard Hat warning sign on the back of the trailer's door.

"Someone probably just tried to kill you," he pointed out again, hoping she'd take him seriously enough to let him hide her someplace safe.

Stubbornly, she lifted her chin. "And maybe someone accidentally placed the wrench too close to the scaffolding's edge. A tremor from one of the concrete trucks could have caused it to fall."

He shook his head as she denied reality. "Look, anything's possible. Maybe it was a coincidence that the wrench fell the moment you took off your hard hat. But maybe it wasn't. I plan for the worst-case scenarios."

"That's a cheery way to live."

"But the point is, you do live."

She shuddered, then straightened her shoulders. "So what's the plan?"

"We hide you."

"And what is plan B again?"

Naturally she wouldn't buy plan A. Oh, no. Alexandra would make things difficult. "We copy the papers Jake sent." He strode over to a brand-new copier and hit the warm-up button. "Is there any way of anyone knowing we used this machine?"

"It's a rental. I believe the machine has a counter and we pay for each sheet of paper that runs through. Why?"

"I don't like leaving tracks. But I suppose we have no choice."

"You honestly think someone would come in here and check with the secretary to see if we used the copy machine?"

"If they are thorough, yes, it's possible—but unlikely. And even if they ask, they'll only know extra pages were printed. They won't know for sure that we made those duplicates."

Alexandra took out the photographs and papers. One of the old black-and-white pictures captured Roarke's attention. He leaned closer. "Can I look at those?"

"Sure." She handed him six or seven pictures.

"This is Colonel Penkowsky."

"Who?"

"An officer of the GRU. Soviet Military Intelligence. He was the highest double agent the CIA ever placed in the Soviet Union."

Alexandra's eyes lit up with hope and excitement. "We should talk to him."

Roarke shook his head. "He's dead."

"You're sure?"

"I attended his funeral in Moscow. It was open casket. I assure you, the man is dead." As he saw the hope dim in her eyes, he tried to give her something to hang onto. "But just his presence in these pictures tells us that your parents must have known the man, possibly worked with him in some operation."

"You think my parents were CIA?"

"It's possible. Do you feel up to making the duplicates while I check around?"

"I guess."

She didn't sound enthusiastic, but he wasn't sure if her reluctance was due to what he'd just told her, how she felt physically, how she felt about him leaving her, or his insistence that they had to go on the assumption that she might not be safe.

As Roarke slipped out the door, he glimpsed her discreetly checking her purse and the weapon he'd given her. *Good girl.* She locked the door behind him without being told. At least she understood safety precautions. But all the precautions in the world wouldn't save her if a team made a frontal attack.

Roarke kept the trailer in view but made a quick perimeter check of the site. Boot prints in the dirt, hand smudges on railings and the scaffolding made it impossible to tell if a worker had just waited for the opportunity to knock off the boss or if someone had accidentally mislaid a tool.

Accidents around his clients made Roarke wary. Accidents around Alexandra had all his senses on alert. Worry weighed down his footsteps. He noted the crews coming back from lunch, some of the men looking at him with curiosity, others murmuring about Alexandra's close call. Discreetly, he scrutinized the men's steel-toed work boots, dirty and concrete-covered, searched the men's hands for calluses. And spied nothing that didn't belong.

Not that he expected to find a killer. If one had been there, he would be long gone.

And yet Roarke couldn't relax. He sensed someone hunting him. Someone out there watching the site.

Waiting to take Alexandra from him.

It wasn't going to happen if his vigilance could stop them. It wouldn't happen if he remained alert. He damn well wasn't going to lose another woman he cared about. And he did care about Alexandra—and not just because she was a client. He liked the way she knew what she wanted and wasn't afraid to go after it. He liked the way she argued with him, standing up for herself. And he liked the way she had kissed him back even when she clearly hadn't wanted to.

He couldn't see anyone suspicious outside the chain-link fence, but he sensed danger with a strength that made him ultra cautious. Roarke held perfectly still and let his eyes search the shadows for movement. Across the street, people strode in and out of a variety of brick and stucco buildings that perched between two skyscrapers. A Chinese restaurant, a lawyer's office, a bail bondsman's blinking neon sign and shop all appeared normal enough.

To the south, the St. John's River flowed almost traffic-free, the scenic water reflecting the city skyline but not providing cover. Semi-trailers parked with construction materials blocked his view of the city to the east and west. The extensive hustle of traffic, honking horns, the occasional police siren and loud stereo systems all sounded normal.

Which didn't exclude a sniper with a rifle scoping

out this site from a quarter-mile away and shooting Alexandra down. Or a businessman holding a semi-automatic behind his newspaper as he sat at the café. A quick stab on the sidewalk. A well-placed knifehand to the neck. Roarke knew all the ways to kill. All the ways to die.

The spot between Roarke's shoulder blades itched as if someone was aiming at his back. But nothing untoward occurred. Gulls screeched overhead. The crews started the concrete pour. And the sun shone brightly with a taunting intensity.

He made his way back to the trailer, knocked twice. Alexandra opened the door, her hands gray from handling not-quite-dry ink. "See anything?"

"Nothing useful." He shut the door behind him. "Are you almost done?"

"Almost." A smudge darkened her chin. "Where do you think I should hide the duplicate papers?"

"Someplace clever."

"Like?"

Roarke looked around the trailer. "Someplace out in the open. Someplace someone could look right at but not recognize what they were seeing."

Alexandra grabbed up a cardboard blueprint tube from a stack in a corner. "How about inside here? We finished this job last year. No one has any reason to open the tube."

"Perfect!" He moved close to her and took half the documents. Their hands touched and static electricity zapped him. "Oops."

Her lips tugged upward as she rolled documents to slip inside the tube. "First you tackle me. Now you're zinging electricity at me. You going to hit me for your next trick?''

''As long as I'm not hitting *on* you,'' he joked.

This time she couldn't restrain a laugh. And he admired her for being able to put aside her frightening experience. She had an upbeat outlook on life that made him feel jaded and rejuvenated at the same time.

Don't get any ideas, bub.

Just because he couldn't forget the fresh taste of her lips or the scent of sunshine in her hair or how amazingly good it felt when she simply held his hand was no reason to think there could be more between them. He didn't mess around with clients. Actually, he hadn't messed around with any woman since Sydney's death.

At first he'd been in mourning. And later, he'd just been too busy with work. It was only since he'd met Alexandra that he realized how much he'd missed talking to a woman, verbally sparring with a woman, looking at—touching—a woman.

But now was not the time to have all these yearnings come back—especially all at once. Especially with the sister of Jake Cochran, who might be a beneficial business contact. Jake could throw lots of business Roarke's way, and Roarke needed those potential referrals if he wanted to continue to work in the States.

While he wasn't ready to settle down behind a white picket fence, he wanted to limit his worldwide roaming. He wanted to work in a country with civilized laws and a justice system that put criminals behind bars.

Perhaps after he completed this assignment, he and Alexandra could go out a few times and discover whether there was more to this attraction between them than lust enhanced by danger. If Alexandra responded to him, he wanted it to be because she was attracted to him, not because their unusual circumstances caused her to behave abnormally. Because eventually the mission would end. He'd rather pursue her once she was no longer in danger.

Right now, he had to keep her safe. Right now he had to concentrate on how to escape the site without anyone seeing them. He needed to keep his mind on business so they could possibly have a future to discover. Together.

As much as Roarke regretted leaving his vehicle and sophisticated equipment behind, he knew better than to depart the construction site in the same car in which they'd arrived. The enemy likely knew their location and could watch the perimeter, waiting for them to leave.

Roarke needed a distraction, a decoy and an alternate ride out. He entered the bathroom and noted the cleaning supplies with satisfaction. A fire in one of the Dumpsters, maybe a contained explosion should draw the eyes of the most vigilant observer for at least a few seconds.

He retreated from the trailer's bathroom with the chemicals in his arms. Before Alexandra could ask whether he intended to go on a cleaning binge, he asked, "Can you find someone to drive my car to my office?"

"Sure."

"Someone about my height with dark hair?"

She thought for a minute. "Won't that put that person in danger?"

"These guys are pros. They don't make a hit until they verify the target. And they don't want me, they want you."

"How are we getting out of here?"

"On the floor of a concrete truck."

"Can't you think of a cleaner option?" She glanced down at her bronze-and-cream pantsuit, already smudged with dirt from when he'd shoved her to the ground. "You sure are hard on my clothes. Around you I'm always getting dirty."

He winked at her, enjoying the image of her getting down and dirty. "I'll let you be on top."

"Very funny." She swallowed a grin.

Glad her sense of humor had resurfaced, he hoped she'd let it out more often. Maybe she thought he wasn't taking the mission seriously enough, but he'd learned a long time ago that the stress of field missions had to be dealt with constructively. Many agents turned to alcohol, dangerously dulling the senses. The stress could kill a man unless he balanced the nerve-wracking spy business with a hobby, a woman, or a sense of humor. The bodyguard business was no different.

Alexandra picked up the phone.

Roarke shook his head. "Don't—"

She paused, the receiver halfway to her ear, frowning as she apparently recalled the information he'd given her about bugs. Twisting the phone cord around her finger, she gave him a thoughtful and somewhat confused look. "Why would anyone bug the office phone?"

"To learn your schedule." No need to tell her that the FBI and the CIA could listen to every phone within four city blocks if someone high enough in the government approved the operation. "Better to be safe. Can you give me a note to pass on to the driver?"

She wrote in a bold scrawl on a pad, one note for the concrete driver, the second for a foreman asking him to drive Roarke's vehicle home. Finished, she handed the messages to him, eyeing the chemicals warily.

"What's up?"

"We need a diversion so we can slip into the concrete truck unnoticed." With the chemicals and messages, he turned to go out the door.

Her fingers gripped his shoulder with surprising strength and pulled him to a halt. "You aren't going to hurt my building?"

"No, ma'am."

"Or any of the men?"

"Not unless they hit me first."

She locked her eyes on his, assessed his intentions, then nodded. "Okay. How long have I got until you come back?"

"Why?"

"I've a few details I should clear up," she gestured to the notepad. "Instructions I want to leave."

"Fine. Just don't use the phone. And don't tell anyone where we're going."

She sighed, tossing the pen onto the desk. "Now there's one thing you don't have to worry about."

"What?"

She played with the tiny diamond earring in the lobe of her ear. "You haven't *told* me where we're going."

He juggled the cleaning supplies and avoided replying to her statement by firing his best believe-in-me grin. "I don't suppose I could convince you that I'm playing this all by ear?"

"A man like you probably has at least three safe houses, five passports and three cars."

"Two and four and two," he admitted, his respect for her rising another few notches. She might be new to the danger game, but she didn't panic, and she kept her brain in gear. And even dusty, she smelled real good.

Too good.

She opened a desk drawer and pulled out a clean trash-can liner. One by one she removed the assorted cleaning supplies from his arms and placed them into the plastic bag. After pulling the drawstring tight, she handed it back to him, her eyes alight with satisfaction and a hint of interest.

She looked as if she might kiss him full on the lips and had then thought better of it. "Go on, already."

"Yes, ma'am." Again he headed for the door.

Again she stopped him. "And Roarke?"

"Yeah?"

"Be careful."

He leaned one hip against the door and looked over his shoulder at her, taking satisfaction from the thought that her warning showed she cared. Especially when it was so obvious that she didn't want to let on how she felt.

He couldn't resist ribbing her. "Worried about me?"

"Naw." This time she let loose her smile, a brilliant smile that made her glow. "Just concerned about my building. Remember, you promised not to hurt it."

He supposed he deserved her teasing. He should

have been annoyed, but he liked a woman who could give as good as she got.

Swallowing back a chuckle, Roarke stepped out into the sunlight and heat, prepared to do battle for this woman. He hoped not even a skirmish would be necessary.

The construction site seemed normal. A gentle breeze picked up the dust and fine particles settled everywhere. Concrete trucks and their drivers waited patiently in line to dump their loads. And with a smooth precision that took years to learn, the crews hustled to even the concrete before it hardened.

Then why did Roarke feel so strongly that something wasn't right? Why did the hair on his neck stand up and sweat trickle from his brow?

What in hell made him so uneasy?

ALEXANDRA OPENED the trailer door and took in Roarke's serious demeanor. No welcoming smile, no ready taunt on his lips. He was all business. He seemed about as uncomfortable as a roofer on a hot copper roof. Eyes bright and wary, weight shifting from foot to foot, he looked as if he expected trouble.

She drew him inside, her stomach knotting. "What's wrong?"

"I'm not sure."

"What does that mean?"

"I'm not sure."

She teased him, hoping to bring back a smile. "What happened to Mr. I-Have-an-Answer-for-Everything?"

If it were possible, his expression darkened. "Someone's out there."

She forgot about teasing him and frowned. "I thought you said you didn't see anything?"

"I didn't."

"But?" she prodded.

She'd never seen him this serious. All business. Until now she'd found it remarkable that he could keep such an upbeat attitude with his life so frequently on the line.

Now she saw another side of him. The vigilant warrior. He wasn't necessarily cold and unfriendly, but was holding back part of himself as he watched out the window and evaluated their situation. Keeping himself at an emotional distance, alert, he was ready to protect her.

But from whom? What could make him so edgy?

She already knew that Roarke liked to feel firmly in control. And that loss of control clearly caused his stress. By reacting with wary silence, he spooked her more than almost any explanation he could make.

However, Roarke hadn't answered her verbally, and she realized he was capable of communicating on many levels. She suddenly understood that he must be operating on pure instinct. He'd gone beyond wary, confident, and observant to another level where he relied on his survival instincts. Even if, on the surface, everything appeared just fine, Roarke wouldn't be a man easily fooled.

This self-assured, independent, tough and assertive man wouldn't be worried without reason. And realizing that made her break into a light sweat and take the weapon out of her purse and click off the safety.

"Put that away," he told her with an abruptness that startled her.

"Okay." She wouldn't think of arguing with him while he was in his warrior mode. This was his area of expertise. And she wanted all his concentration focused on the enemy, not on arguing with her.

"The concrete truck is on the way over. I told the foreman to instruct the driver not to park but keep it rolling."

"You tell me when."

"We go when he's less than two feet from the trailer door. You first. Keep your head down below the dash."

She understood that he wanted to hide their getaway from any interested observers. If the truck kept moving, he hoped that no one would realize what they were doing. The concrete truck would provide cover and they could sneak away unnoticed—if the driver didn't accidentally run them over...

Fear escalating, but determined to do nothing to hinder their chances, Alexandra slung her purse strap over her shoulder and picked up her briefcase. She felt a little better when she remembered that they'd hidden the duplicate copies in the cardboard blueprint tubes. Her biggest worry was that someone would stop the driver to question him and they'd be caught trying to leave. However she knew Aaron was busy with his engineering crew and Tyson had gone to check over the plumbing, so neither man should miss her until she was long gone.

Roarke's diversionary explosion made her jump. Flames shot out of a trash can. No one would be hurt. No damage would occur.

With all eyes presumably occupied on the flaming trash can, she fought to keep her nerve as Roarke first opened the trailer door, then advanced and opened the passenger door of the concrete truck as it rolled closer.

"Ready." He paused. "Go."

She rushed out the door.

He didn't wait for her to climb inside by herself, giving her an unexpected boost from the rear. She tumbled onto the dusty seat, barely remembering to keep her head low.

Right on her heels, Roarke dived onto the floor-boards, sending up a cloud of dust and closing the passenger door behind them. The entire procedure couldn't have taken two seconds. The driver shifted into another gear and the truck accelerated a few miles per hour.

"Turn right the way you always do at the gate," Roarke instructed the driver.

"Will do."

Curled on her side, Alexandra looked up awkwardly at the driver. The middle-aged, overweight man shook his head at her but gave her a thumbs-up.

The truck's windows were closed, the air-conditioning blessedly welcome, so she didn't fear anyone hearing her and felt free to speak.

"Appreciate your helping us out," she told the driver, raising her voice over the noisy engine.

"No problem. You should get one of them restraining orders against your old boyfriend, ma'am. Then you wouldn't have to resort to this kind of stuff."

Restraining order? Old boyfriend? She figured Roarke must have told the driver another story, and she marvelled at his inventiveness. While she had doubts that all his precautions were necessary, she'd much rather play it safe—even if she did ruin another outfit.

Cement dust stained the seat, her clothes and her hair. On the floor, Roarke must be filthy. Yet, he didn't move or complain. Instead, he'd taken a telescopic device that looked like a miniature periscope from his pocket and peered out the window through the eyepiece from his position on the floor.

They headed through the city streets for several minutes before the driver slammed on his brakes.

Unprepared for the sudden stop, Alexandra tumbled onto the floor, her purse and briefcase going with her. Roarke let out a grunt as she landed on top of him.

Both doors of the cement truck jerked open.

Alexandra looked up and into the barrel of a deadly-looking gun being held by a white man of medium build with thinning brown hair. He appeared to be in his fifties, and his eyes were cold and deadly.

"Get out, lady," the gunman growled. "Keep your hands up," he instructed the driver. Then he peered down at Roarke. "You move and I'll shoot her."

Alexandra did as she was told. While her purse remained slung over her shoulder, she'd left the briefcase behind. She thought she heard the slight sound of Roarke shifting her briefcase under her seat and took her time climbing out to the deserted side street.

Another man grabbed her, yanked her hands behind her back, tied them with tape and shoved her into a car trunk. Less than a minute later, the men shoved Roarke in next to her.

The trunk's lid came down and left them in darkness. Packed like sardines and spooned on their sides, her chest to Roarke's back, Alexandra was very glad she didn't suffer from claustrophobia.

Until this moment, she hadn't had time to be scared. They'd been taken from one vehicle to another with such precision and swiftness, she'd barely kept track of what had happened. But now that they were enclosed in the darkness, fear made her shake and her teeth chatter despite the heat.

As the car drove away with them inside, she was thrown against Roarke. "What happened to the concrete driver?"

"Don't worry about him. He must have been in on their scheme."

"He's a regular driver, not a criminal."

"So they paid him off."

"How did they know we would try to get out that way?"

"These guys are pros. CIA."

CIA? Oh, God! What the hell had her brother gotten her into by sending her those papers?

Chapter Seven

Roarke raised his aching hands behind his back, wondering if he could raise them high enough for Alexandra to bite through the tape. But there wasn't enough room. Lying with his knees to his chest, almost in the fetal position, his legs were cramped, his arms ached and his fingers were going numb from the tight wrist bindings. Alexandra had to be feeling the same discomforts, but she hadn't complained.

He'd have to think of a way to free himself. Meanwhile, he gave Alexandra more information about the organization he knew so well.

He whispered to prevent his voice from carrying to their kidnappers. "On a sunny day, the agency can direct a satellite to read the date off a dime lying in the dirt. Our escape could have been spotted from overhead. Or the trailer could have been bugged before we arrived."

"You shoved my briefcase under the seat?"

"Yeah." He'd been pleased she'd exited the truck so slowly, covering his movements, and now he knew why. She'd read his intentions all along. She might be untrained, but she had a knack for undercover work.

"I don't think the driver noticed. But right now I'm more concerned about getting out of here."

It was hot enough inside the trunk to make him sweat. Her breasts rubbed against his back, her hips intimately pressed against his buttocks. And every time the car bounced or turned, her body stroked his enticingly. Now was not the time to notice how her breasts felt. Nor were these already cramped quarters the place for his groin to swell, but that part of his anatomy had a mind of its own. However, not all the heat stemmed from the friction of two bodies rubbing together. The sun was turning the trunk into a steam-room.

"I still have my purse and your gun."

"Good." He was thankful that she was thinking clearly.

He'd come loaded for war, but he'd been taken by surprise and stripped of his weapons. He really wished he knew exactly who they were up against. Although these men had to be CIA-trained, they could be rogue agents. Or on an unofficial assignment from a higher-up with his own agenda. Either way, Roarke felt sure the operation wasn't legitimate. The CIA didn't kidnap American citizens and stuff them into car trunks. He took some comfort from the knowledge that, while he didn't stand a chance of hiding a woman in the U.S. for any length of time with the full resources of the CIA behind the search for her, a few rogue agents could be defeated with luck and a lot of planning.

The assessment of their tactical situation took even less time than the analysis of their position. "When they frisked me, they took my backup weapon, my knife and my belt buckle, which has a razor blade hidden inside.''

''There's manicure scissors in my purse. Think they'll cut through the tape around our wrists?''

''One way to find out.''

Alexandra twisted and squirmed, pressing and rubbing against him to free her purse strap from her shoulder. She used her knees to bring the purse to his tied hands. He opened the bag and rummaged for the scissors. Touched metal.

''Damn,'' he swore softly. ''I dropped them.''

She held still, giving him as much space as possible. ''You'll find them. Take your time.''

''Okay.''

''You…have…them?''

''By the tips.''

''Wait until…we finish…going around this…corner.''

''All right. Slow and easy this time.'' Cutting himself free in the jouncing car with his hands tied behind his back required the skills of a contortionist and the concentration of a determined mind.

While he worked the scissors, she stopped talking. Her breathing turned ragged and he didn't like how she sounded.

''Straighten up if you can. You'll breathe easier.''

''Are we…running…out…of air?''

''That's the least of our worries. We can release the air in the spare tire if we have to. I'm more concerned about the temperature.''

''Hot,'' she agreed.

Stifling. The Florida sun was baking through the trunk and roasting them. Without water, they could dehydrate within fifteen minutes.

While Roarke kept that grim possibility to himself, he used the tiny manicure scissors on the tape around his wrists. Beside him, Alexandra seemed limp.

"You still with me?" he asked her softly.

"Don't feel too good."

He cut through the last of the tape. "I'll cut you free in a minute. First let me see what I can do about the temperature in here."

"Always knew...being next to you...make me hot. Isn't...what...had...in...mind," she joked, her voice weak.

"Hang on. Don't talk. Don't move. Save your strength." With his hands free, Roarke found a flashlight in the trunk and flicked it on. "Good news. There's a toolbox."

Alexandra's breathing sounded like raw gasps. She needed air. Fast.

Still she whispered. "You're good with...hands."

He doubted she knew what she was mumbling. Found nothing amusing in her rambling comments. He had to get the temperature down while he could still think coherently.

Inside the toolbox, he found a rusty screwdriver and went to work on removing the rear taillight. It wouldn't be a lot of ventilation but it could help, and just might make the difference between living and dying. If he could remove both taillights and kick or punch out the reflector panels, he'd create a cross current of air to help even more.

And maybe a cop would notice the missing taillights and pull the car over.

Sweat dribbling down his forehead into his eyes,

Roarke's damp hands kept slipping on the screwdriver. But finally he removed enough screws to pull the taillight into the trunk. He knocked out the reflector with his fist.

Turning himself around proved impossible in the cramped space. So he bent over and eventually he pulled in the second taillight, too.

The outside air rushing through the trunk helped bring down the temperature and gave them fresh oxygen to breathe. While it was still very warm, he no longer thought he might dehydrate beyond a point where he could think.

He wished he could change positions with Alexandra and let her have more of the cool air but no way was that possible. Nevertheless, her breathing seemed a little better and she no longer rambled incoherently. While he couldn't switch places, he could roll until he faced her. He nudged her onto her side and cut her wrists free.

"How're you doing?"

"You sure know how to show a girl a good time."

Another joke? Maybe she hadn't been incoherent before. Maybe the lame jests were her way of dealing with discomfort and stress. My kind of woman.

But she was not his woman—she was a client, he reminded himself, wondering if he was thinking as clearly as he'd thought. Especially with the wild idea that had just popped into his head.

He flicked off the flashlight to give her some privacy. "Would you please remove your bra?"

"EXCUSE ME?" Alexandra must have heard him wrong. Between the wind rushing through the trunk and the bits of dust being kicked up and swirling around, she'd surely misheard him. "I thought you asked me to remove my bra."

"I did."

While she knew Roarke couldn't be making a pass at her in the car's trunk, she didn't like the idea of removing her underwear—even in the dark. With the cool air flowing through, her thinking cleared, and she easily recalled all the rubbing she'd done against his back. Even now her breasts still seemed a bit tender. To remove her underwear in such close quarters and receive more sensual stimulation was the last thing she wanted. Accidental or not, she had had enough friction in her sensitive spots, thank you very much.

While the flashlight had been on, Roarke had no longer looked like Mr. Perfect. Sweat beaded his dark skin and his hair was damp with sweat and slicked back on his head. He sported a smudge of dirt from his cheek to his chin. Cement dust covered his clothes, but, though not perfect, he still looked good enough to pose in one of those working-man's commercials.

That she'd been turned on by his looks while her life was at risk annoyed her to the point of crankiness. She had to force a calmness into her tone that she didn't feel. "Mind telling me why you want me to undress?"

As usual, Mr. Silver Tongue had an answer for everything. "I want to push your bra out the taillight hole and use it as a flag."

"Couldn't we use your shirt?"

"Which article of clothing do you think will draw more attention?"

There was no winning an argument with him. Without another word, she unhooked her bra and slipped it off from beneath her shirt, a maneuver difficult at any time, but while lying on her back she had to struggle.

She finally handed it to him, glad he'd turned the flashlight off. Not that her bra was unusual. Plain, white cotton with underwire cups. Not in the least erotic. So why did she feel embarrassed? "Here you go."

"Thanks."

With her bra gone, the air cooled the perspiration on her chest. And yet she felt twice as vulnerable. Although she no longer expected Roarke to attack her at any moment, she didn't trust her own reactions to him. She didn't want to notice his looks every time she glanced his way. She didn't like having to peer through the pretty-boy image to see what he was truly like. It was difficult enough to get a handle on this man without his distractingly outrageous good looks.

She knew deep down that not every good-looking man took advantage of women. She knew deep down that judging Roarke by his appearance and comparing him to Patrick was unfair. Yet old habits died hard.

One moment Roarke could be so light and teasing. But when he suspected danger, he closed down the charisma and charm, revealing a far darker side to his character. This side of him alarmed her more than the civilized one, because, while he would protect her, she found his intensity unnerving.

He'd taken the bra and started to slip it out the taillight when the vehicle slowed, then halted. The car engine kept running, but they could hear a door open and shut.

She felt Roarke's movement and heard the rustle of cloth on metal as he yanked the material back into the trunk. She held her breath, wondering if the trunk would open, wondering if their captors had spotted the missing taillights.

Roarke lay on his side, his head crammed up against one opening which blocked most of the light. Without the air rushing through from the car's forward progress, the trunk's temperature began to increase again.

Lying quietly, she picked up the sound of coins dropping and someone punching buttons. At a pay phone. They'd stopped to make a phone call.

Clearly their captor had no worries about them overhearing the conversation. Why should he? Even if he didn't know they had a gun or that their hands were free, they were trapped. Alexandra hoped the trunk didn't become their coffin.

She shuddered at the grim thought. Her parents would have no idea what had happened to her. She could be one of those people who just disappeared and was never heard from again. And what would happen to her beautiful building? Someone else would take over, change her plans and probably ruin her clean design.

Frustration welled up inside her. She wasn't ready to die. No matter what happened when that trunk opened, no matter how weak she felt, she vowed to fight. If they were going to kill her, she wanted to take one of them with her.

The savage turn of her thoughts shocked her. She didn't think of herself as a vicious person, but having her freedom taken from her, being stalked for some reason she couldn't fathom, had brought out her fighting instincts. She didn't want to die, yet even if she survived, she would be different. Just knowing how far she might go to stay alive had changed her in an elemental way.

The man's words drifted to her clearly from the phone booth. ''Boss, we got the package. Where do you want me to deliver it?''

It didn't take a rocket scientist to figure out that she and Roarke were the package. And that these men were taking them to meet at least one more bad guy—their boss.

Next to her, Roarke turned and whispered. ''I see a sign. We're at the corner of Main and Ninth. If anything happens to me and you get away, tell the FBI these jokers made a phone call from here.''

''Okay.'' Main and Ninth. She wouldn't forget, but she sincerely hoped Roarke would be around to do the talking. Not only would she feel tremendous guilt if they couldn't escape together, she would miss him.

Somehow, her dislike had turned to like. She was not immune to his easy courage and his blatant charm. And, while she needed to be truthful to herself, she still didn't know how he'd changed her opinion of him. He was still arrogant, bossy and determined to have his own way. But he was also thoughtful, considerate and a fine man to have on her side in a dangerous situation.

''Yes, it's the right package.''

She held her breath to hear better.

''Hey, I killed her father, I can do the daughter, too. No problem.''

Oh, God!

At hearing the driver so casually mention killing her father, Alexandra stifled a scream.

Oh, God. Not her father. Not the man who'd adopted her and taken her into his home, caring for her as if she were his own. He couldn't be dead.

And yet their captor had spoken as if it were a done deal. She couldn't imagine her easygoing father with his potbelly and twinkling blue eyes no longer part of this world. Her throat tightened and tears slipped down her cheeks.

And her poor mother. Her parents had been childhood sweethearts, married in their teens. Her mother had lost her husband and now she would lose the only daughter she'd ever known.

Shocked and full of sorrow, Alexandra didn't notice that Roarke had gathered her into his arms. She only knew she welcomed the comfort of his shoulder and needed the touch of his strong fingers brushing back her hair.

Even the man who always knew the right thing to say had no words to offer her now. The black emptiness of her soul threatened to overwhelm her. Roarke's arms grounded her and made her feel still connected to this world.

Anger swelled in her heart, battling for space with her sorrow. How dare these men kill the father she loved? What gave them the right to play God? To take away the most precious gift of all?

She didn't hear the rest of the phone call. Lost in her thoughts and roiling feelings, she barely noticed the discomfort of the heat. Didn't register the temperature dropping as the car pulled back onto the road.

She lost track of time, her thoughts swirling with

thoughts of horror and grief and anger and revenge. Yes. Revenge. She wanted the SOB who'd murdered her father dead—or at least behind bars for the rest of his miserable life.

"I'm sorry," Roarke whispered. "So sorry. I lost a woman I loved in Africa. Her name was Sydney."

She could hear the pain still in his voice and, despite her own grief, her heart went out to him. "What happened?"

"She died during a terrorist bombing of the embassy." He drew a deep breath. "We were engaged one day, and then the next day, she was just gone. I couldn't work. I couldn't go on doing the same thing day in and day out as if she were still alive. It was as if my dreams died with her."

"That's when you quit the agency?"

"Yes."

She had no words of comfort to give him, just held on tightly, the grief over her father so fresh, she thought it would tear her apart.

Roarke smoothed hair off her forehead. "I didn't realize your father would be in danger."

"It's not your fault. How could you have—" She stiffened at another awful thought. "My mother?"

"She must be fine. He didn't mention your mother."

Roarke sounded so confident, but was he putting on an act to comfort her? "You're sure?"

"Yes."

Alexandra wondered if her fear and sorrow were making her suspicious. She couldn't bear the thought of losing both of the people that meant the most to her. "But why didn't Mom call me?"

"You weren't home, remember?"

She swallowed the lump in her throat. "Roarke, I have to go to her. She needs me, now that..." She couldn't say the words. Couldn't stand to think of saying a final goodbye at the funeral, of the days ahead without her father.

She had to think of something else. Anything else or she would go quite mad. She needed to act, but they remained stuck in the car trunk. So the first order of business had to be escape. Her voice might not have been steady, but she forced the words past the sorrow clogging her throat. "What's the plan?"

Gentle, he brushed away her tears. "When they open the trunk, listen for me to grunt. I'll wait until after you climb out, then can you keel over?"

"Sure." Keel over? The way her cramped legs felt right now, she might not even have to fake it. "But suppose they don't open the trunk?"

The car started to move again and he shoved the bra through the hole. His voice turned grim. "We shoot the lock."

She didn't understand his reluctance to use the gun. "Why can't we shoot it open now?"

He sighed and shifted his arm to pillow her head. "It's not like in the movies. A bullet could ricochet in here. And it's just as likely to fuse the lock tight as bust it loose."

"So that's a last resort?"

"Yes."

Finally Roarke was treating her as a partner, explaining what she needed to hear. But concentrating was so hard. Memories of her father kept interfering with her thoughts. His proud face when she'd announced she wanted to be an architect. His support through the difficult college years. His offer of financial help when she'd gone out to start her own firm. Every step of the way, he'd been behind her, emotionally, financially and, most importantly, giving her unconditional love. Her eyes welled with tears but she kept talking, hoping to ease her pain. "And plan B?" she prodded, hoping he had one, suspecting he had plans from A to Z.

This time he sounded even more reluctant to speak, actually hesitating before speaking. "When they open the trunk, I take them by surprise and start shooting."

She fished inside her purse and handed him the gun. "Why isn't that plan A?"

"Because they'll shoot back."

"And?"

"And you'd be in the line of fire."

"And if I keel over, I'll be safe on the ground?"

"Safer than on your feet. I want you to roll or crawl for cover first chance you get."

Now she knew why he'd spoken to her like a partner. He wanted her cooperation. "But then I won't be able to help you."

He hugged her tighter for a moment. "Don't think I don't appreciate the thought, but if you're out of the line of fire, it'll leave me free to do my stuff."

"Your stuff?" He said the words with a lightness that shot a ripple of unease through her. Never before in her life would she have felt so at ease with a man who considered death a part of his job. Yet Roarke had gently held her while she'd cried. Those hands that had smoothed away her tears had surely taken lives. And she was becoming comfortable with the idea. If in self-defense Roarke happened to bring down her father's murderer, she wouldn't regret it.

He admitted as casually as if he were talking about the state's drought, "I'm skilled at hand-to-hand combat."

She heard the confidence in his tone, his faith in his abilities and yet she couldn't keep back her concern. "Won't the bad guys know that stuff, too? And won't they outnumber you?"

"I'll be better. Now quit worrying over me and conserve your strength."

"Roarke?"

"Yes?"

"I'm glad it was you that Jake picked to protect me." Her brother couldn't have chosen anyone smarter or more dedicated or more capable. She didn't blame Roarke in the least for their current predicament. He'd warned her not to go to work and she hadn't listened. She only wished that he wouldn't have to pay for her mistake with his life.

As if reading her thoughts, he held her a bit tighter. "I could have done a better job of protecting you."

"There's nothing you could have done," she insisted, knowing she spoke the truth.

"I should have stopped you from going to work."

"I made that choice." She shook her head, wishing she could see his expression to know if she'd eased the guilt she heard in his voice.

"My point, exactly. I shouldn't have allowed you to make the decision."

"Really?" He had an odd way of looking at things. Taking responsibility for her actions.

"I knew better. You didn't."

She sensed this wasn't the first time he'd accepted blame that wasn't his. But no matter how broad his shoulders, he couldn't hold so much guilt inside without it casting shadows that would darken his future. Oh, he did a good job of hiding the guilt beneath his pretty face and charming manners. She recalled the information her reporter friend had given her, and she'd bet the penthouse of her new building that Roarke blamed himself for the disaster in the embassy where so many people had died. Where his fiancée had died. Especially since he'd quit shortly thereafter.

Although the darkness wove a web of intimacy around them, she didn't have the right to dig into his past. And then the car ground to a halt. Roarke yanked her bra back into the vehicle and handed it to her. She stuffed her underwear into her purse, her thoughts focused on the immediate future.

"Pretend your hands are still tied behind your back," Roarke instructed.

As two doors clicked open and footsteps approached the trunk from both sides of the car, Alexandra slipped her purse strap over her shoulder. While she squirmed into position, her hand knocked against the screwdriver. She clasped it tight and wedged her hands behind her back.

"Remember, wait for my signal. Wait for me to grunt," Roarke reminded her.

A key scraped against the lock. Alexandra tensed and squinted, expecting bright sunlight.

The trunk opened.

Chapter Eight

Roarke kept his gun in his hand but hidden behind his hip. While he couldn't shoot from that angle, he could move into position quickly if he had to. As the trunk opened, he breathed a sigh of relief that their two abductors had been joined by only one other person.

The third man stood about six foot two, wore a coat and tie and an Agency-regulation haircut. From the way his two cohorts deferred to him, he was clearly in charge of the operation, but Roarke saw him watching nervously over his shoulder and guessed he wasn't the top dog. Possibly more foes were coming. Maybe the top dog himself from the way the new man acted.

They'd been taken to an empty warehouse with a rusted roof, cobwebs and old oil spills on the floor. The place not only appeared deserted, but as if no one had worked here productively in years. Empty gasoline drums and trash were too far away to provide cover. The open doors at either end of the building were too far to make a run for freedom.

Roarke assessed their position and worried over the lack of nearby cover. He saw no adequate place for Alexandra to hide, and his adrenaline pumped.

With two weapons pointed at Alexandra and himself, opening fire on the enemy would probably get them killed. So Roarke slipped the weapon into the waistband of his slacks. As the men yanked him up and out of the trunk, he waited for a better opportunity to attack.

"They have the papers on them?" the man in the suit asked, tapping his foot with impatience.

The two underlings exchanged glances as they roughly lifted Alexandra from the trunk. "What papers?"

"No one told us about any papers," the other agreed. "We had orders to bring them here. Mission completed."

The guy in the suit uttered several blistering curses. "Check her purse."

Roarke tensed. Time was running out. He had to take out two men before the third could pull the trigger and before more showed up. Not the easiest of assignments, but he had no choices left. Once the men discovered Alexandra no longer had the papers they wanted, they would have no reason to keep anyone alive, which was standard operating procedure for illegal groups like this one. These men couldn't afford to have accusations thrown their way, so they didn't leave behind witnesses who could talk.

Roarke decided to take out the guy in the suit on the first blow. He needed to strike silently to gain the precious seconds needed to keep Alexandra safe.

Apparently, the suited man wasn't a field agent or he would have kept his weapon aimed at them instead of loosely pointed at the cement floor. He might be built like an ox, but Roarke suspected the man pushed paper and read intel for a living.

As one underling reached for Alexandra's purse and placed himself between her and the other underling, Roarke made his move, knowing it might be the best chance they'd get.

Roarke grunted, sending his signal to Alexandra. Simultaneously, he fielded a roundhouse kick to the boss's chin. On target, the ball of his foot connected, and the big man's head snapped back, his neck broken. He let out a soft, "Oof," then collapsed.

Spinning, Roarke took down the second opponent with a deadly knifehand to the throat before his first foe hit the ground. But as Alexandra dropped to the ground, the man after her purse reacted. Like a cat, he spun, aiming his gun at Roarke, his eyes sharp, his expression deadly.

Roarke looked into the other man's eyes, and time slowed. He actually saw the man's finger tensing on the trigger, ready to pull. Roarke's weapon was still inches away from position to shoot.

He braced for a bullet, his exquisite sense of timing telling him he'd lost this round. He'd failed big-time. And he'd pay with his and Alexandra's lives.

As his opponent's gun fired, the man's eyes widened in surprise, then he stumbled and let out a yowl of pain, throwing off his aim. The bullet meant for Roarke's brain whizzed by his ear.

From the ground, Alexandra had stabbed the man in the ankle with a screwdriver! Roarke didn't give their foe another chance. He aimed and shot before the man could get off another round. A tiny hole appeared between his sightless eyes and the stench of blood and death permeated the warehouse.

Slowly Alexandra climbed to her feet, her whiskey-colored eyes wide with fear, her olive-toned skin pale as she took in the three dead men. Wobbling unsteadily on her feet, she went paler as she stared at the screwdriver still sticking out of the man's ankle.

"Are you okay?" she asked Roarke.

"Thanks to you."

At the opposite end of the warehouse, a car drove inside, its headlight surrounding them with a stark brightness that left them as vulnerable as deer in a hunter's scope.

They had company. Top Dog had showed up, but all Roarke could see of him through the lights was his shiny white head. Top Dog was bald. And likely furious that his prey were escaping, his unit members dead.

Having so many operatives in one place and the expense of the operation briefly crossed Roarke's mind, but he couldn't stop and ponder. The reinforcements weren't the friendly kind.

While Roarke wanted to console Alexandra, they didn't have time for the niceties. Roarke scooped up the car keys and a gun that had fallen to the pavement. He pressed the gun into Alexandra's hand as he rushed her toward the car. "Get in. We need to get out of here."

"Duh!"

That she still had a sense of humor amazed him. Roarke had directed teams in the field, but as an agent, he'd usually worked alone. He now realized the value of having a partner, even an untrained one, especially one like Alexandra.

He skidded out of the warehouse, took the only dirt road and hoped it didn't lead to a dead end. While he suspected they were in the industrial area, he'd never been in this part of town.

As he drove, grateful for the dust kicking up behind him, Alexandra reached across him and yanked and secured his seat belt before fastening her own.

"Thanks." He risked a glance her way, glad to see her color returning to normal. "You have any idea where we are?"

"A man who asks directions? How unusual!"

"Very funny. There's a street sign up ahead. See if you can read it."

"It's too dirty to read." She opened the glove compartment in search of a map and let out a curse of disappointment.

He checked the mirror and behind them the other car held its distance, neither gaining nor retreating, but at least staying out of shooting range. He squinted to make out the driver's features, but all he could see was the man's bald head.

Roarke couldn't afford to make a mistake and drive into a dead end, or the other car would be on him like a Love Bug on wet paint. "We're coming up to a paved road," he told Alexandra. "Which way you want to go?"

"There's no street sign."

"Left or right?"

"Now you let me make a decision—when I have absolutely no idea where we are."

"Choose."

"Right."

He sped around the corner, knowing that while he had to focus on keeping the car on the road, she'd pick up visual cues he wouldn't. They accelerated past several warehouses, a junkyard of rusting cars and a dilapidated gas station that looked as if it hadn't been open in the last decade.

"Can you pull over and hide behind that pile of steel?" Alexandra pointed.

"Can't." Roarke shook his head and veered around a giant pothole. "They'll notice an immediate lack of dust and figure out we stopped."

Alexandra looked back over her shoulder. "We're slowly pulling away. But we can't race through the city streets without endangering innocent lives."

Roarke made a series of turns and finally struck pavement and a two-lane road. Taking advantage of better traction, he pressed the pedal to the floor, and the car's powerful engine responded with a surging leap in speed. A glance at the speedometer showed they were fifty miles an hour over the speed limit.

Where was a cop to give him a ticket when he needed one?

Roarke passed several cars and, as the traffic increased, he was forced to slow. Knowing that the car chasing them faced the same problem did not decrease his concern. As long as Alexandra remained in danger, he couldn't afford to make another mistake.

The death of her father had brought sad memories of his own. He knew what it was like to lose someone he loved. And just as he'd blamed himself for Sydney's death, Alexandra would feel guilty for not warning her father, for not making sure he knew he was in danger, for accepting the package from her brother. A million "what ifs" would go through her mind. He knew all too well what was going through her head because he'd been there. He also knew that what anyone else said didn't make a damn bit of difference.

So he'd said little, just held Alexandra while she'd sobbed in his arms, giving what little comfort he could. At least in his case he'd had the consolation of tracking down the terrorists, seeing to it that they would never kill again.

To escape his morbid thoughts, he focused on his driving. His need for speed made him take calculated chances, weaving in and out of traffic, passing other cars and trucks at every opportunity. If Top Dog called in a satellite to track him, Roarke needed to drive the car under cover—but nothing was available, not a shed or garage or bridge.

Beside him, Alexandra tensed, one hand braced against the door, her face pale, but she didn't protest the risks he took, completely aware that if they were caught, they died.

Roarke spied signs directing him toward a major highway and cut through an intersection as the traffic light turned yellow. Hoping the chase car would be caught at the red light and buy him an extra sixty seconds, Roarke headed onto the on-ramp, arbitrarily picking north.

"There!" Alexandra pointed.

Her sharp eyes had spotted a faint trail from the ramp through short grasses to a low-lying area of oaks. If they could make it to the cover of the trees, not only would they evade their pursuers, they wouldn't have to risk a high-speed chase on the open highway.

Without hesitation, Roarke followed Alexandra's suggestion and pulled off the ramp. The grass wasn't as lush on the path. The drought had turned almost everything brown, disguising the trail. The only difference was that here the grass was a tad sparser than on the rest of the sandy area. Other vehicles had come this way but not for a long time. He just hoped that when they reached the trees, they'd find enough clearing space between the trees to hide the entire vehicle.

As shade enclosed them, he edged the car deeper into the wooded area, unwilling to take a chance of chrome, glass or mirror glinting and giving away their location. Finally, he turned off the engine.

"Now what?" Alexandra asked softly.

"We wait."

"I don't like waiting."

He took her hand. "You did great back there in the warehouse. Without your help…"

At the look on her face, he immediately realized his mistake. He shouldn't have reminded her of the death they'd left behind. She wasn't accustomed to that kind of violence.

"You did what needed to be done," he assured her as he pulled out his gun and checked to make sure it was fully loaded. If their pursuers found them, he needed to be ready, but his actions also gave Alexandra a moment to collect herself. Although the car engine was off, he'd left the keys in the ignition and counted on it starting immediately if they had to make a run for it. He checked the bullets and slammed home the clip with a proficiency that had become second nature to him.

Alexandra pulled out the gun Roarke had given her,

but held it listlessly on her lap. Roarke suspected she still felt horror and guilt over the killings, but he could think of nothing to ease her inner turmoil. Every person had to deal with the aftermath of violence in his or her own way.

So he remained silent, simply taking the gun from her and checking the load before handing it back, making sure the safety was on. She barely noticed. He ached at the pain he saw in her eyes, wanted to pull her into his arms, but not only did the car's bucket seats make comforting her difficult, he couldn't afford to let down his guard.

While in all likelihood their pursuers were speeding down the highway, either north or south, they might double back and spot them. Roarke needed to remain alert, his mind on her safety. Later, if she needed help, she could talk to a counselor about her state of mind.

New agents often needed a few sessions with a professional to sort out their feelings when they came in from the field after their first violent encounter, even though these agents were as prepared as the Agency could make them for wet work, killing. Alexandra had nothing to be ashamed of. For a civilian, she'd acted with uncommon valor when it counted. With the proper training, she'd make an excellent Agency recruit, yet he knew that she much preferred her buildings.

Back at the bank site, her face had glowed with enthusiasm as she'd supervised her skyscraper. Her eyes had lit up, almost sparkling with pleasure, during the concrete pour. He could only imagine how she'd feel when the skyscraper towered over the cityscape, dominating the riverfront with its clean lines and graceful curves.

He hoped she would be there to see it. He also doubted she understood how dangerous returning to the site would be. This time he couldn't let her talk him into letting her go back. No matter how spectacular the building might be when finished, she couldn't risk her life over steel and glass.

He didn't want to overwhelm her with more problems, especially now that she was feeling so vulnerable, still coping with the news of her father's death and her own part in the death of their kidnappers. As the minutes passed, her color returned, although a sadness remained, haunting her eyes and tugging at his heart.

"I need to get to a phone and call my mom," she told him, her voice almost breaking. "She's going to need me."

He understood her obligation to her mother, but he also knew how much danger Alexandra would be in if she insisted on attending her father's funeral. Not to mention the danger they could bring to her mother. The date and time and place of the ceremony would likely be placed in the newspaper where anyone could see it. Top Dog was out there somewhere, hunting them and Roarke suspected the man wouldn't stop until he got what he was after.

Roarke kept his concerns to himself. One step at a time. Right now, he needed to make sure they lost their pursuers. "Let's give it another half hour."

"These people who murdered my father want to kill me, too." She looked at him with eyes too wide, too pain-filled for him not to feel a twinge of guilt.

He should have done a better job of hiding her. "I won't let them hurt you."

"They already have. They took away the most important man in my life. And I don't even know why."

He had no answers for her, but the frustration and sorrow in her tone turned his stomach into one giant knot. "The key has to lie in those papers your brother sent you."

"Maybe we should just give them the papers. Keeping them wasn't worth my father's life."

"You can't know that."

She tilted her head back against the headrest and closed her eyes. "What could be so valuable?"

"I don't know. Before, I only suspected your biological parents once worked for the CIA, now I'm almost sure of it."

She jerked upright. "Why do you think so?"

"Sometimes the CIA uses couriers who are simply American business people or tourists. But those men after us are Agency-trained."

"And?"

"The important documents were carried only by agents."

"There's more, isn't there?"

"I'm Agency-trained. With all the P.I.s your brother has working for him across the state, he could have hired anyone."

"But he chose you. Why?"

"I suspect because of my background with the Agency."

She considered his line of reasoning but didn't immediately accept it. "But he didn't tell you that, did he?"

Roarke shook his head. "He didn't even know for sure that you would be in danger. He just wanted to take precautions."

"I'm glad he did. And I hope he's all right."

"While you made copies in the trailer, I checked with Harrison. Your brother's assistant still hasn't heard from Jake, and he assured me he wouldn't forget to call us the moment he hears from him."

The intelligence world was a small one. Roarke had heard about her brother, and, after Jake had hired him, he'd done a little checking. Unlike Alexandra, her brother had never been adopted. He'd grown up in foster homes. With no help from family, he'd not only survived the state system, he'd grown tough there. But unlike so many unloved youngsters, he hadn't taken to a life of crime. Instead, he'd founded one of the premier private investigation firms in the country.

"Your brother has a reputation for taking care of himself."

"What do you know about him?"

"Not much." He hesitated to tell her how rough her brother's life must have been as he'd bounced from foster home to foster home. "I work in a small world of professionals and word gets around. Using skills he learned in the military, your brother built his P.I. firm up from nothing. He has an excellent reputation. I'm looking forward to meeting him."

Her expression turned wistful. "So am I. Did you know I also have a sister out there somewhere?"

Roarke hoped Jake had found protection for the other sister, too. She would need it if Jake had sent another copy of the materials to her. But right now, he could only worry about his client. "Jake didn't mention your sister. Actually, we spoke for less than a minute. In retrospect, I think he kept the conversation short to avoid a trace.''

Alexandra looked at the clock on the car's dash. ''Roarke, I have to call my mother.''

''I know. Let's go find you a pay phone.''

WITH SHAKING FINGERS, Alexandra dropped coins into the pay phone that Roarke located at a convenience store. She had to be strong right now for her mother's sake. No matter how awful she felt, she had to be there for the woman who had loved her and had raised her.

Every year at this time, her parents moved north to escape the summer heat. Each summer, they rented a house or apartment in a different part of the northeast. Last year, they'd stayed in Cape Cod. The year before her dad had taken up fishing off the Hudson River. This year they'd rented a cabin on Lake George in upper New York State.

Eyes filling with tears, Alexandra could barely read the numbers in the book of personal numbers she always carried in her purse.

''Hello?'' her mother's cheerful voice rang through as clearly as if she was right next to her.

''Mom, I'm sorry I couldn't call sooner—''

''—It's fine dear, I'm sure you're terribly busy with your first skyscraper.'' Why was her mother prattling on about Alexandra's building? For God's sake, her father had died, been murdered, and her mother sounded as if she hadn't noticed. Alexandra made herself listen, her hopes rising as her mother continued, ''Your father and I are so proud of you. Just last week over a bridge game, your dad was bragging to the

Simsteads about your building. They may not invite us back after we cleaned them out—''

"How's Dad?" Alexandra interrupted, clutching the phone so tightly her hands shook. Was it blind hope? Or was it possible those men had been mistaken? Could her father still be alive?

"Here, I'll put him on and you can speak to him."

"Hi, sweetie."

"Dad!" Her voice choked up at the familiar voice. Roarke heard her scream of joy and squeezed her shoulder, no doubt worried she might faint from the shock. "You're okay?"

"Of course I'm okay. Your mother and I are visiting Fort Ticondaroga this afternoon. Tomorrow we're taking a boat out to an island for a picnic lunch. Honey?"

"Yes, Dad?"

"What's wrong?"

"I was worried about you, that's all." She covered the phone's mouthpiece and whispered to Roarke, "Should I warn them? Do you think they're in danger?" When Roarke shook his head, she took his word. She wasn't thinking clearly right now, and if Roarke thought her parents were safe, then they probably were.

She and her father exchanged a few more words and she told him not to worry if he didn't hear from her for a while. "Love you, Dad."

"Love you, too, sweetie."

"Give Mom my love."

She hung up the phone. "My father's alive. He's fine." Dazed, pleased, lighthearted and very, very confused, she looked to Roarke for an explanation, knowing she hadn't misunderstood the man who'd said they'd killed her father and were about to kill her.

From the expression on Roarke's handsome face, she could see he'd already figured out the puzzle and left her way behind. Normally, she'd be upset that she still hadn't caught on, and he'd figured it out first. But she was so filled with joy after talking to her father that she didn't care if Roarke's IQ was double hers. Nor did she care that he was shooting her one of those arrogant, thousand-megawatt smiles, knowing he was as genuinely pleased as she was.

"So?" she asked.

"What do you mean, so?"

"So what am I missing? What haven't I figured out that has you so smug?"

"Nothing."

"Don't give me that, Mr. Perfect P.I. You're holding out on me. With you, that's a given."

His brows came together in a scowl, but his twinkling eyes gave away his amusement. "Was that an insult?"

"It's the truth. You always hold something back behind that pretty face."

"Pretty face? That's a definite insult."

She touched his rib cage, gratified to learn that he was extremely ticklish. "Do I have to torture you to get you to talk?"

He grabbed her hand and pulled her close. Too close. They stood chest to chest in the convenience-store parking lot while other customers bought gas, used the rest rooms and made calls from the pay phones. She gazed into his perfectly blue eyes and suddenly had trouble drawing another breath.

His eyes had darkened with a longing that tugged at her heart. Not desire for her, but for another woman. The woman he'd lost in Africa. When she'd believed her father was dead, had her grief brought up terrible memories for Roarke? And now that she'd learned her father was alive, had he been rethinking how happy he would have been if he'd found his fiancée alive in the bombed building? Alexandra couldn't read his mind, but she suddenly felt ashamed for teasing him. Felt guilt over her own happiness.

She could see he wanted to share her delight, but he remained silent. Perhaps she was reading him wrong. He never gave her much to go on. "What's wrong?"

She seemed to be asking that question a lot lately.

"I didn't want to intrude on your good fortune at finding your father alive. But I think I know the answer to the puzzle."

"Well, tell me, already," she demanded impatiently.

Chapter Nine

First, Roarke insisted that they return to the car. Roarke hated to put a dent in her happiness, but he had to tell her that he'd figured out the puzzle. "That man wasn't referring to your adopted father but to your biological father."

"My biological father?" Her hand on his forearm heated him all the way up to his shoulder and down to his feet.

"It's the only thing that makes sense."

"I was told my father had died in a car accident."

"Maybe the 'accident' was arranged."

"Why?" As they left the pay phone, she squeezed his arm with intensity. She looked to him for answers, and he wished he had more information to give her. He also wished he felt free to lower his head and kiss her again, hold her in his arms again. He recalled from holding her inside the car trunk how well they fit together—her head snuggled against his shoulder, her breasts softly rubbing his chest, her sweet breath fanning his face.

He ignored the heat of his thoughts and walked her back toward the car. "I'll bet the answer is in those papers your brother sent. We need to go to the cement company and retrieve your briefcase from under the seat of that truck.''

She slid into the passenger seat and glanced up at him, and he'd bet she remained totally unaware of how she affected him. ''I don't suppose it's safe to go back to the construction trailer and retrieve the spare set?''

''Nope.''

Her nose scrunched a little as she frowned. ''You don't want me to go back to work?''

''That's a given.''

''But, but...''

''Your safety has to come first. Your building will have to wait.'' He started the car. ''I'm sorry.''

''You really are.'' She stared at him, her eyes wide.

''Are what?''

''Sorry.''

He squirmed internally before he answered. ''Don't you think I know what it's like to give up a dream?'' The moment the words popped out of his mouth, he knew he shouldn't have said them. He'd aroused her curiosity, and he didn't want to talk about the past, about how naive he'd once been, about how little his efforts had changed the world.

''Don't you dare.''

''Huh?'' Had he missed part of the conversation? Lost track while his thoughts were focused on the past? He pulled onto the highway, heading toward the city.

''Don't you dare think of using that silver tongue—''

Silver tongue?

''—of yours to avoid an explanation.''

He shook his head and flashed her an I-don't-know-what-you-mean look.

"And don't try any more of those charming smiles to distract me."

"Why would I want to distract you?"

"To keep from telling me about yourself. You're so good at evasion."

"I am?"

She didn't bother to answer his question, recognizing it as simply another evasive tactic. "What was your dream?"

"When I was a kid, I wanted to be a fireman," he teased, knowing she wouldn't give up.

"And I wanted to be an astronaut." She scowled at him. "Turn right at the next exit. That road will take us straight to the cement company." She glanced at the dash. "It's four o'clock. Most of the trucks should have made their last run by now."

"Good. How many cement trucks do you think the company has?"

"Over a hundred. Why?"

"I'd like to check them without anyone spotting us. The more trucks, the more difficult it'll be to remain undiscovered."

"It was truck number 131."

"You remember?"

"I also remember that once again you're trying to avoid my question."

She wasn't going to let him off the hook. Damn, the woman could be persistent. And even through his irritation, he wanted to kiss her. Even if she could be annoying. Annoying could be…sexy. Erotic. Splendid.

Damn it, he should never have kissed her the first time, because now he knew what he was missing.

While he admired her ability to notice and remember the number on the cement truck and take an hour off their search time, he didn't like to talk about his past. He didn't like to remember the friends he'd lost. Especially when every memory always went back to Sydney and his failure to protect her.

Yet, for some reason he wanted to share his past with Alexandra. "I dreamed of peace in Africa. I dreamed of a democratic continent where children didn't go to bed hungry at night. A continent where AIDS didn't decimate entire villages. A land where all people could be free of tyranny. The first step in achieving that dream had been to counter the terrorism that prevented other nations from sending help."

To her credit, she didn't laugh. "You thought you could make a difference?"

"All it would have taken was enough money. After the Cold War ended, we could have done so much."

"You didn't get the money?" she guessed.

"Less than one percent of the American budget goes to foreign countries," he couldn't keep the bitterness from his voice.

To his surprise, she defended the congressional actions he found so inconsistent. "It's human nature to want to help those at home first."

"Then what the hell were we doing over there? Why send Americans overseas to work and not give them the funding to do their jobs?"

"Isn't a little help better than no help at all?"

Their conversation ended, for now, when she

pointed to a sign up ahead. "That's the cement company. What's the plan?"

"We find the truck, take the briefcase and leave."

She nodded her understanding. "Suppose it's locked?"

"I'll pick the lock."

"Suppose the security guard stops us?"

He pulled into the dusty yard and parked under a Visitor sign. This late in the afternoon many of the office workers had already left. Construction people started work early. Most of the cement trucks were parked in neat rows. "Just tell anyone who asks that you think you might have dropped an earring in the truck when you spoke to the driver earlier today."

"And if we run into the driver?" Alexandra asked.

"Let me worry about him." Roarke hoped they did. It might be unprofessional, but he'd enjoy confronting the cement truck driver who'd probably taken a bribe and almost gotten them killed.

As soon as he and Alexandra openly headed for the cement trucks, the security guard noticed. After telling him who she was, Alexandra gave him the prepared story, and the helpful guard escorted them to the truck in question.

Now they had a problem. Roarke hadn't expected the guard to remain with them. They'd told the man Alexandra was in search of an earring, but if she found the briefcase instead of a piece of jewelry, he'd be suspicious.

The guard, Alexandra and Roarke had reached the parked truck, which was halfway down a row, when the driver from this morning walked right up to them. All Roarke's protective instincts fired at once. He stepped between Alexandra and the driver who'd betrayed them.

The driver peered around Roarke at Alexandra, concern in his eyes. "Are you all right, ma'am?"

"No thanks to you," Roarke muttered, already suspecting that the man had a ready excuse for his traitorous behavior.

"It's okay, Joe," the driver waved away the security guard. "I'll help our guests."

"Like you helped us this morning?" Roarke itched to plant his fist in the driver's face. He didn't care that the man was ten years older than him and out of shape. He only remembered how close he'd come to losing Alexandra due to this man's collaboration with the enemy.

The driver couldn't meet Roarke's eyes. "I'm so sorry about that. Those men threatened my wife and kids." He twisted a battered hat in his hands. "They said if I didn't do what they wanted..." The driver placed his hat on his head and hurried toward the cab of his truck. "I didn't tell them about your briefcase."

"Is that so?" Roarke muttered. Not only didn't he believe the driver's claim, he looked around the cement yard with suspicion. If the driver was now lying and had told their pursuers about the briefcase, a trap could snap shut on them any moment.

But Roarke didn't see anything suspicious. Drivers pulled their trucks into the yard, washed them with a hose and then parked the trucks. Soon after, the drivers walked to the parking lot for their own vehicles and left by the front gate—all perfectly normal activities.

"I was hoping you'd be back." The driver pulled

the case from under the seat and offered it to Alexandra. "Everything's still there. I didn't open it."

Alexandra took the briefcase with a warm smile for the driver. "Thanks."

"You won't report me to my boss, will you, ma'am? I can't afford to lose this job."

"You're lucky she doesn't report you to the police," Roarke threatened, not because he intended to carry through, but because he wanted to put a good scare into the driver, unbalance him and extract information. "Did those men who hijacked us show you any identification?" Roarke asked.

"No, sir. But they didn't just threaten."

"Sure," Roarke scoffed.

The driver dropped his voice. "They had my wife. They let her talk to me on the phone."

Alexandra frowned at Roarke, clearly questioning the particulars of the driver's story, too. "But you picked the truck, didn't you, Roarke? How could anyone know which truck we would take?"

Roarke realized his mistake. He hadn't picked the driver himself. He hadn't guessed they were being watched so closely or anticipated that his foes would guess his next move. "I asked a foreman to send over a driver."

"They switched trucks. This isn't my normal vehicle," the driver explained, again twisting the cap in his hands. "They told me I would drive any vehicle that Ms. Golden requested. I'm sorry. I didn't mean for anything bad to happen. They told me if I warned you or did anything suspicious they would hurt my Mary."

"I understand." Alexandra was more forgiving than

Roarke. But at least he no longer had the urge to hurt the man. The driver might be telling the truth.

As Alexandra and Roarke walked back to the car, Roarke pulled the papers out of the briefcase and dumped the case in a trash bucket.

"Hey, that's leather!" Alexandra protested, her mahogany eyes burnished in the setting sun.

"They might have a bug planted inside."

"But the driver said—"

"We already know we can't trust him."

"Roarke, they were threatening his wife."

"So he says. It's more likely they slipped him a hundred bucks."

"But he didn't give them the briefcase," Alexandra argued, with irritating logic.

All along he and Alexandra had believed their pursuers were after the briefcase. But their pursuers could have found the briefcase and discovered that it hadn't contained what they wanted. They could be following Alexandra and Roarke right now, hoping they'd lead them to whatever they were ultimately after. Or the driver could have been telling the truth. Either way, he didn't want to take chances with Alexandra's life. "It never pays to be too careful."

"Especially when it's not your briefcase in the trash." She shook her head at him, a tiny smile turning up the corners of her mouth.

He placed his arm over her shoulder and walked her to the car. "We need to ditch this car and find a place to hole up for the night."

"Let's go someplace nice," she suggested. "My treat."

AFTER THEIR ROUGH DAY, Alexandra felt as if she'd been on an emotional roller coaster. She wanted to relax over a good meal, soak in a bubble bath and consider her options. Roarke drove by a parking lot where he kept a spare vehicle.

"How many cars have you got stashed all over town?" she asked him.

"Several. I keep spare cash in the trunks with a gun and a few necessary tools."

Once again she realized how lucky she was to have Roarke helping her. He knew how the CIA operated and could outsmart them at their own game.

They switched cars and headed toward the beach, then south along A1A. The two-lane highway wound past beachfront homes overlooking the Atlantic Ocean. The area had recently become more built up, but it hadn't lost the laid-back attitude that characterized beach communities. Teens with surfboard racks on their cars parked along the road and walked over to the beach. Families barbecued on their porches, taking advantage of the shade from their houses as the sun set over their yards.

"Where are we heading?" Alexandra asked.

"Eventually, St. Augustine."

She glanced at him, watching his face carefully for telltale reactions. "You want me out of town?"

"St. Augustine has some excellent restaurants."

He was back to evading her questions again.

"What do you mean by eventually?"

"I wanted to leave you somewhere safe, then go back to the phone booth where we overhead those men talking."

"Ninth and Main? But why go back?"

"Maybe our friends left fingerprints, although finding them after so many hours may be difficult. But the phone company might trace the calls made from that location."

So he planned to stash her somewhere and then go play private investigator. She'd wanted to argue but needed his full attention, which she couldn't have while he kept driving. When she spied a few empty lots, cars parked along the road and a path leading to the beach, she stretched. "How about a walk?"

He shot her a puzzled look, but one that said he'd humor her to keep her happy, even if he thought she was making a peculiar request. "A walk?"

"Along the beach. To stretch our legs," she added a smile to her invitation. He wasn't the only one who knew how to use a smile to his best advantage.

Roarke parked, and they strode past saw palmettos, sandspurs and crabgrass toward a softly sloping beach. Waves gently lapped the beach, leaving wet crescents in the sand. A catamaran surfed through the waves, the two teenagers aboard seemingly oblivious to anything but one another.

While she kicked off her shoes and happily dug her toes in the sand, Roarke didn't let down his guard for a moment. She'd glimpsed him checking his gun as he walked her across the street. He scrutinized every person on the beach—man, woman or child—with a thoroughness that led her to believe he could describe them later, if he had to, with deadly accuracy.

She didn't bother using small talk to lead into the topic she wanted to discuss. "Ever since I thought my father had been killed, I've been thinking about those documents."

He picked up a flat stone and skipped it across the waves. "And?"

"I don't want them."

"You don't know what you have."

"Exactly. So I won't miss them if they're gone."

Without judging her, willing to hear her out, he turned and stared into her eyes, for once not trying to influence her with his perfect features. "What do you mean *if* they're gone?"

"Why can't we just give the documents to the people who want them?" His eyes darkened, a muscle in his jaw clenched, but she didn't give him time to voice an objection. "Look, you said I shouldn't risk my life for a building, a project I've worked toward all my life. I've put my heart and soul into that steel and concrete and metal—yet, you're right. It's not worth my life. But neither are those papers. I vote we give them back."

When she paused for breath, he arched a brow. "Are you done yet?"

"I'm making sense. I don't want the papers. Let those guys have them." She gestured wildly with her hands. "I don't want to live my life looking over my shoulder. I don't want to risk the lives of people I know. And for what? Some diary that was written before I was born."

"Your mother's diary."

"I don't mean to seem calloused, but I never knew her."

"She gave you life."

"My real mother, the mother I love, is vacationing on Lake George right now. And my father is happily fishing. The man who killed my biological father is back in that warehouse—dead. You can't give me one good reason to keep running.''

''What about the man who gave the order to kill your father? I might have taken out the hit man, but should his boss go free?''

Alexandra groaned and dropped to the sand. She sat facing the ocean, letting the setting sun warm her back, her face lifted into the salt breeze. She should have felt peaceful. Instead her stomach roiled with unanswered questions. ''You don't know that the man on the other end of the phone gave the order.''

Roarke squatted beside her, still alert, still scanning the beach for any possibility of danger. ''I'll have a better idea who we're up against after I get the phone company's records and dust the phone for prints.''

She groaned again. Talk about a one-track mind. The man didn't have the word *quit* in his vocabulary. ''You think it's safe to backtrack?''

''That's why…''

''You wanted to leave me.'' She dusted some loose sand off her hands. ''Well, that's not going to happen. My brother hired you to protect me, and you can't do that unless you're close. Real close,'' she repeated his own words back to him and watched his eyes change from surprise to annoyance to a hot blue flame of desire.

Desire? Surely she had to be mistaken. She must look a wreck. Cement dust clung to her clothes. She'd torn her blouse, hadn't reapplied her makeup in…she glanced his way again to check him out.

He looked sexy as hell in his slacks and shirt. In the fading light, his features looked darker, his bluest of blue eyes even brighter. She decided he'd look good wearing rags. And even better in nothing at all.

"I'll stay as close as you want me to be," he agreed with a predatory gleam in his eyes that would have rocked her back on her heels if she'd been standing. Since she was sitting, she simply swayed against him and knocked him from his comfortable squat onto his butt.

"You aren't taking me seriously," she complained.

His smooth voice turned husky. "How seriously do you want me to take you?"

"Would you stop? Just stop."

"What?"

"Making everything I say into some kind of sexual innuendo."

"I'm sorry if I'm making you uncomfortable," he sounded sincere and yet she sensed him holding back a chuckle.

"I'm not uncomfortable. *Annoyed* would be a better adjective for how I feel about you."

"Then you won't mind if—" with a proprietary gesture, he placed his arm over her shoulder "—I do this."

She damn well did mind. Her pulse rate increased by at least ten beats per minute. And her temperature had to be up with all the heat he sent through her.

How like a man to stop a serious conversation by sidestepping the issue and flirting. How like him to distract her with his over-the-top sensuality.

His hand made tiny, torturous circles along her arm, shooting another flare of heat to the back of her neck. He started edging it slowly toward her breast, and her breasts swelled longingly. She could no longer tell herself she didn't trust this man. She could no longer hold his good looks against him. She could no longer hold back her own needs and wants and desires.

She cocked her head up at him, letting him see the invitation in her eyes. "I think we should find a hotel."

Chapter Ten

"First, we need to find that phone booth," Roarke replied, finding the enticement in her voice irresistible. Almost.

He had to get a grip on his emotions. Now, when they might find some clues if he kept his mind on work, was not the time to let her distract him. So why couldn't he cease thinking about how good it would feel to pull Alexandra into his arms and kiss her senseless, or how incredible she made him feel when she looked at him so trustingly, or how much he felt like a spark on one of those Fourth of July bottle rockets?

Keeping his brain focused on business had never been so difficult. When they'd left the cement yard, he should have driven straight to the phone booth. His protective instincts kept battling with his need to solve this case. However, he had to focus on his primary job—protecting Alexandra had to be his first priority. She wouldn't be safe until he learned who was after those papers and why, and letting her tag along while he investigated was too dangerous. So he'd wanted to hide Alexandra and return to search for clues.

Clearly, she didn't want to be left behind. And, in

truth, she might be safer with him. Then again, that he *wanted* to keep her with him might be influencing his judgment. And a man in the field couldn't start second-guessing himself.

Roarke needed a clear mind right now. But how could he think clearly when all he wanted was to take off Alexandra's clothes, piece by piece, and explore every inch of her? Slowly. Ever so slowly, he wanted to make her melt.

"What are you thinking?" she asked as she brushed the sand from her palms and stood.

"Why?" he asked, having no intention of telling her that his mind had strayed so far from business.

She arched one delicate brow, her eyes filled with curiosity. "You had this really awesome gleam in your eyes. As if relishing the challenge ahead."

Her ambiguous words could refer to the challenge of winning her trust enough so she'd allow him to make love to her until dawn. Or she could have referred to the task ahead. He had no trouble choosing which topic he preferred to talk about. "I need to find another pay phone."

"Some day, you're going to answer my questions," she muttered in frustration, and her words brought a small grin to his lips.

A grin he didn't dare let her see. She was already much too good at guessing the direction of his thoughts. She didn't need any extra hints from him.

Roarke headed back toward the city and stopped the car at the next pay phone to call a friend in the FBI. "Hey, Carleton. How'd you like an opportunity to do some field work?"

Carleton groaned. "My wife just fixed my favorite

dinner of fried chicken, mashed potatoes with gravy and fresh asparagus.''

"So I'll owe you one."

"You already owe me ten. For that sheik in Baghdad. The politician in Panama. Hey, do you think I've forgotten about that Irish—"

"Not on the phone." Normally Roarke would have let his friend complain and elaborate, but they both knew who owed whom. Roarke had saved Carleton Jamison's FBI unit. In thanks, Carleton's wife Natalie had named her first-born son after Roarke.

"Meet me at the phone booth at Main and Ninth with your gear. You do still know how to use it?"

"Very funny. What happened to your kit?"

"Lost it when I got carjacked."

"Yeah, right. With your luck, there's a lovely lady involved."

"Of course. I'll introduce you if you like. Give my love to Natalie."

"I'm on my way."

"Hey, Carleton."

"Yeah?"

"Keep your eyes open."

During the thirty-minute ride to meet his friend, Roarke explained to Alexandra that Carleton worked in the FBI's Jacksonville forensic lab, searching for clues on dead bodies to track down drug runners. His friend worked mostly nine-to-five and stayed home on weekends with his family.

Roarke parked next to the phone booth on the totally deserted street amid abandoned warehouses, apartments and junkyards. "Alexandra, this is Carleton."

"Nice part of town to bring a lady, Roarke," his old friend teased, then his eyes widened as he took in Alexandra's slim beauty. "You're lucky I'm married, ma'am. Or I'd steal you away from him."

Alexandra raised a brow. "A faithful husband? I like that in a man."

Roarke kept his voice low. "You two don't need to be getting cozy. Alexandra, take that gun out of your purse. Shoot only as a last resort." He turned to Carleton. "I need prints. Some time today might be good. I need the identity of the man who used this phone earlier today."

"You after him?"

"He's dead," Roarke's tone was grim. "I want his boss."

Carleton took out his fingerprint dusting kit. "Was he wearing gloves?"

"Nope. I had a clear view of his hands from the trunk."

"Too bad you couldn't see the number he dialed."

"I'll get that information from the phone company. He made the call at half-past noon."

Carleton held up his hands. "Don't tell me any more. I don't need to know."

Roarke knew his friend ran a squeaky-clean operation. Carleton never broke the law. He never even skirted the edges of the law. And he slept well at night. But then he had Natalie and three charming rugrats at home.

"Getting anything?" Alexandra asked while the two men worked slowly, paying special attention to the receiver.

"We're getting too much."

"There are prints all over," Roarke explained. "But we'll run them through a computer file and see who has a record. He leaned over Carleton's shoulder and used a tool to jimmy the coin box.

"Hey," Carleton protested. "That's stealing."

"Not if I put the coins back after you take prints off them it isn't."

Carleton shook his head. "Alexandra, I should warn you, this man makes his own rules."

"He's saved my life twice. Maybe three times," Alexandra said softly. "That counts for a lot."

"You don't have to pay him back by falling for his smooth-talking charm," Carleton advised her. "I didn't."

Roarke chuckled, accustomed to Carleton's frank talk but curious about how Alexandra would take the remark.

"That's good advice, Carleton. I'll remember it." Clearly Alexandra wasn't offended. In fact, she seemed amused. "I take it from your warning that you don't think Roarke is husband material?"

"I didn't say that."

"You better be damn careful what you say," Roarke threatened.

Carleton wasn't the least bit intimidated. "Roarke hasn't been ready to take on a woman since Sydney died. But I think you've rattled his cage."

"I'm going to put you in a cage if you don't shut up," Roarke complained, but somehow he couldn't put any sting into his words. Carleton must have caught the vibes between Alexandra and him the moment he'd seen them together.

And Alexandra was good for him. Dreams that had

died were starting to come back to life. He was once again thinking about his future. The question was what he intended to do about it.

ALEXANDRA LIKED Roarke's friend Carleton. The man had an innate honesty about him that appealed to her. That Roarke had such a friend corroborated her own good opinion of her bodyguard and increased her trust in her own judgment about men—which had been sadly lacking since she'd parted with Patrick.

Carleton had headed to his office to compare the fingerprints they'd found in the phone booth with the FBI's extensive files. Roarke would call his friend from a pay phone every hour or so for an update.

Meanwhile, she and Roarke were heading to the phone company to see another of Roarke's contacts. Alexandra had been surprised to learn that while regular office hours were nine-to-five, many of the utility's operations stayed open around the clock.

When Roarke pulled into a drive-through at a fastfood place, Alexandra realized that her stomach had been rumbling for hours. He handed her a burger, fries and a chocolate shake, and she bit into the food with relish, not minding in the least that if she'd gone to St. Augustine she could have been eating gourmet food in one of the city's fine restaurants. She'd much rather be here with Roarke.

Watching him work intrigued her. He was so selfcontained, so confident and smooth. Observing him thinking on his feet and unraveling the mystery surrounding them was akin to watching Tiger Woods putt or Pete Sampras serve at Wimbledon. Roarke was a professional who played for the highest stakes—their lives. And he wore the responsibility with style, comporting himself with the confidence of a superstar athlete.

After their very long day, he didn't look at all weary. He still held his posture ramrod straight, his eyes still checked the car's rearview mirror every thirty seconds, and he did his job while noticing the tiniest of details about her.

He handed her a napkin. "You have ketchup on your bottom lip."

She wiped her lips and popped a French fry into her mouth, chewed and swallowed before speaking. "How do you stay so alert?"

"Habit."

"Aren't you feeling sleepy?" she asked curiously.

"A catnap might be nice."

Catnap? She'd like to sleep for twelve solid hours. Roarke had unusual stamina, and she hoped she wouldn't slow him down too much.

He pulled into the facility and at the gate handed the guard identification. The guard waved them right through, asking no questions.

She gazed at him curiously. "Come here often?"

"Regularly enough to know that if I slip the guard a hundred-dollar bill, he'll let me inside."

"If we get caught, are we going to be arrested?"

"Probably." The prospect of spending a night behind bars didn't seem to faze him. "Are you wishing you'd stayed in a safe hotel?"

"I'm wishing you might tell me, in advance, what kind of trouble you expect."

He parked the car, walked around and opened her door. "I don't expect any trouble. Who's going to catch us? The guard who just took my money? I don't think so.'' He took her hand and tugged her toward a side door. ''It should be unlocked if Carleton remembered to call Rosa for me and tell her that we're coming.''

''Rosa?''

''She's a sweetheart. Has a voice like an angel.''

She could tell by Roarke's tone he was really fond of the woman. She could also hear from his teasing words that he wanted her to be jealous. No doubt Rosa would turn out to be sixty-five years old.

But again, Roarke surprised her. He opened the door and led her down a brightly lit hallway to a door marked Records. He knocked twice and a beautiful Hispanic woman let them inside. Lush curves matched a luminous smile and huge, wide-set brown eyes. She wore a plain blue dress with only a delicate gold crucifix around her neck for flash, but even in rags she would have been knock-down gorgeous.

The woman threw her arms around Roarke's neck and kissed him right on the mouth with a happy squeal. ''It is about time you came to see me.''

Not the least bit embarrassed at the sultry greeting, Roarke placed his arm over the woman's shoulder. ''Rosa, I'd like you to meet Alexandra Golden, a client of mine.''

Alexandra held out her hand to shake.

Rosa ignored it and embraced her, kissing each cheek in the European manner. ''I am happy to meet you, Alexandra Golden. What can I do to help?''

Alexandra sensed a story here. The beautiful woman had the manners of an aristocrat, the regal bearing of royalty, yet she worked in the phone company? With

Rosa's looks, she could have modeled in Paris or New York. But now was not the time to ask questions. And surprisingly, Alexandra didn't experience the slightest twinge of jealousy. While she suspected that Roarke had helped this woman in the past, and Rosa would help Roarke any way she could, she appraised him through the eyes of a fond sister, not a lover.

"You have been working too hard again? *Si?*"

Roarke nodded, his blue eyes piercingly honest. "Perhaps. Someone is stalking Alexandra. We need phone records from a booth on Ninth and Main from between 11:00 a.m. and 1:00 p.m. today."

"Let me make you a printout. While I work, help yourselves to some coffee." Rosa pointed toward a kitchen area for employees that was currently vacant.

Alexandra led the way and poured coffee into throwaway cups. She took a seat at a table opposite Roarke and pushed sugar and cream his way. But like her, he preferred his coffee black.

She sipped the coffee and looked at Roarke over the brim of her cup. "Where did you meet Rosa?"

Roarke stared into his coffee, his voice dark, yet even. "I helped break up a sex-slave ring in Central America. She had been taken captive by a general."

"You freed Rosa?" Alexandra guessed.

"We fled out the front and were fortunate to escape. Another agent and Rosa's twin sister had died trying to go out the back."

Alexandra could hear the sorrow in his voice and realized anything she might say would seem trite. Roarke took failure hard. Any failure. She supposed his caring so much made him very good at his job, yet she wondered if he slept well at night. Did nightmares rise up to haunt him?

"Rosa could find work on a Paris runway as a model. Why is she working here?"

"She's still hiding. She can never go home. Never see her family again. She may have to hide for the rest of her life."

"The general?"

"Is obsessed with finding her."

"And where is this general now?"

"He's vice president of his country, and supreme commander of the army." Roarke's tone implied he wished he could put the man six feet underground in an unmarked grave.

The click of Rosa's heels interrupted their conversation. She swept into the room, a paper fluttering in her hand. "As usual, you are very lucky. Only two phone calls were made during the timespan you specified."

Rosa handed the printout to Roarke who stood and kissed her on the cheek. "Thanks, you've been very helpful."

"You are welcome, my friend. Be careful, and go with God." As they walked out of the building, Roarke looked at the phone numbers. Alexandra leaned over his shoulder and read along with him. The first called a taxi. But the second call went to Rome.

"Rome? I don't understand." No credit card or phone card had been used. She didn't remember a huge number of coins dropping into the phone. "Did that man put enough money into the phone to make an international call?"

Roarke shook his head. "His call was rerouted through several satellites."

"So the call can't be traced?"

"Not with the equipment available to Rosa."

Alexandra walked to the car and stopped to look at Roarke. "What kind of criminals have the ability to reroute calls?"

"Sophisticated ones."

"What are you saying?"

"Some government agencies routinely reroute their calls and encrypt the messages."

"You mean like the military?"

"Or the FBI or the CIA."

A shiver of fear shot down her spine as she climbed into the car. All along he'd kept telling her they might be up against a government agency, but she hadn't really believed him—until now. The phone printout had just confirmed their suspicions. More than ever, she wanted to give up the documents before someone was killed, but from the look of determination on Roarke's face, she knew she had her work cut out to convince him to see things her way.

"We need to make one more stop before we turn in for the night."

She bit back a groan of protest. "Where are we going?"

"Just to a pay phone to call Carleton. Let's see if those fingerprints turned up anything useful."

"GOT ANYTHING GOOD for me?" Roarke asked Carleton.

"Five hits."

Roarke held the phone receiver so Alexandra could hear, too. "Tell us more."

"The first two guys are in the minor leagues. Then we've got an ex-con wanted for murder and rape, another for grand larceny. And then it gets real interesting."

Roarke could hear the excitement in Carleton's voice, and his hopes of solving this puzzle rose. "Our last fingerprint came off a quarter and belongs to one Simon Smithee."

"So?"

"He worked for the Agency twenty-five years ago."

Roarke figured Smithee was one of the men he'd killed that afternoon. Obviously Smithee had quit the Agency for more lucrative work. It happened sometimes. Good men went bad under the pressure. Roarke didn't understand Carleton's excitement.

"And here's the kicker."

Next to him Alexandra held her breath.

"My records say that Smithee died during a wet assignment in the Soviet Union over twenty-five years ago."

But Roarke had killed him that morning!

"So who was the guy in the phone booth?" Alexandra asked.

"Ah, that's the million-dollar question," Carleton told her. "If Smithee had died two decades ago and someone else took his identity, the fingerprints wouldn't match. So either Smithee faked his death, and he was still alive to make that phone call earlier—"

"—or your records are wrong," Roarke finished for him.

"It's always a possibility," Carleton admitted cheerfully. "I tried to check who he worked with and which division he'd been assigned to and came up with classified codes I can't break. Sorry."

"Hey, you've been a big help. Thanks." Roarke hung up the phone, his mind swirling with endless possibilities. Twenty-five years ago, the Agency's record-keeping system was in the process of being switched from paper to computer. The likeliest possibility was that Smithee had died and the records were wrong. And yet…Smithee would have been an operative at the same time as Alexandra's parents. A connection too coincidental to ignore—especially since her mother's papers had included a picture of a known CIA spy. Besides, Smithee had bragged about killing Alexandra's biological father.

"Don't you have contacts in the CIA who could check on this Smithee guy?" Alexandra asked as they drove toward a safe hideout Roarke had used before.

"Yeah, but I don't want to set off any alarms. We don't know if this is a legitimate operation or someone freelancing on the side. And since we don't know who is involved, asking the wrong person could get us killed."

"So now what do we do?"

"Let me sleep on it. I do still have some friends I trust. I'm just worried that if they start asking questions…" Roarke ran a hand through his hair. "I wish I could talk to your brother. Compare notes."

Alexandra's voice filled with worry. "Do you think it's odd that he hasn't shown up yet?"

"Not if he's undercover. I wouldn't worry about Jake. He knows what he's doing."

"How can you be so sure?"

"He hired me to protect you, didn't he?"

His comment, as he'd intended, brought a smile to her lips. "That's what I like about you."

"What?"

"You're so modest." She leaned back in her seat and closed her eyes. "Where are you taking me?"

"Camping."

Her eyes popped open. "Camping?"

"Camping. To spend a night outdoors." He defined it for her, a teasing lilt in his tone.

"Are you talking about camping—like in a tent?" She didn't sound pleased. In fact, she sounded downright miffed.

"It'll be too easy for someone to find us at a hotel—"

"—which would have hot and cold running water."

"—and I'm much too tired to drive across state lines into Georgia—"

"—I could drive," she volunteered.

"—and so are you."

When she didn't utter any further protests, he swallowed a grin of approval. Still, he couldn't resist teasing her a little more. "Haven't you ever gone camping?"

"Once."

From her tone he figured the episode had turned out to be a complete disaster. "Tell me."

"I must have been about eight and had a friend over for the night. We camped in the backyard."

How dangerous could that have been? "Did you get

mosquito-bitten?'' he teased her, thinking about his snug tent. The only thing he'd let bite her tonight was him.

''Mom and Dad cooked us hamburgers and we had a nice fire. We roasted marshmallows over the flames and burned our tongues on the gooey insides. We took our flashlights with us to our sleeping bags and zipped up the tent. We told each other ghost stories and fell asleep.''

''Sounds peaceful enough.''

''Well, it was until I woke up in the middle of the night with a creature standing on my chest.''

''What kind of creature?''

''A raccoon must have smelled the marshmallows still sticking to our faces. I shoved the raccoon off me, and my friend was bitten by the raccoon's mate.'' Her tone became grim as she finished, ''She had to go through the series of rabies shots. It was pretty awful.''

''Hey, I'm sure it was. But this tent is raccoon-proof. And snake-proof.''

''How's that possible?''

She was very tense, and he wanted her to relax. Tonight, they would be safe. No longer tempted to tease her, he explained. ''A grateful client deeded me the use of his lakefront property for my lifetime. Before I got it, he used to bring his motor home there to camp for the winter. His wife wanted a deck built to overlook the lake and the spring. He built the platform on telephone poles ten feet off the ground.''

''We're going to camp on top of the platform?''

''And I never bring food in there.''

She nodded in acceptance. ''It'll feel great to bathe in the lake and wash this cement dust off.''

"That can be arranged." He grinned to himself when she didn't mention the lack of a swimsuit.

"It would sure be nice to have clean clothes…for tomorrow."

"I might be able to arrange that."

She reached over and patted his leg, just above the knee, shooting a bolt of heat straight to his groin. And she knew exactly what she was doing to him. "You're good at arranging things."

"I'm good at lots of things," he agreed, willing himself not to speed down the highway and show his impatience. Already sensing that tonight with Alexandra would be special, he wanted to take his time. As much as he might like to follow his base instincts, he had no intention of pulling over onto the shoulder, ripping off her clothes and making frantic love to her.

He needed a moment to cool down, but that might not be possible as her fingers rested lightly on his leg. "There's a washer and dryer there."

"You have electricity?" Surprise raised her voice an octave, and she moved her hand slightly higher up his leg.

"My client spent his winters there and his summers in Canada. He liked to camp. His wife liked the comforts of home, so he built this giant garage where I store supplies, food and clothing and weapons. Maybe you should wait to see the place before you jump to conclusions." He could see he hadn't yet banished all her apprehension over camping. But he would. He intended to keep her far too busy tonight to think about anything but him. "I've ridden out a hurricane on a couch in the bunker."

"Maybe we should sleep there."

"You haven't seen my tent."

She gave him a saucy look. "That's not all I haven't seen."

Chapter Eleven

As Roarke drove onto a dirt road and under hundred-year-old granddaddy oaks draped with Spanish moss, Alexandra felt the day's tension easing from her shoulders. Although she longed to check on the progress of the bank building, she reminded herself that she had good people working for her, people who cared as much as she did about the project's successful completion.

Roarke turned off the dirt road, stopped and got out of the car to unlock a gate. She drove the car through, and he locked up behind them before rejoining her. "This is where the property line begins."

"How much farther?" Alexandra asked, more to make conversation than out of real curiosity. She'd rather be at a hotel with Roarke, but she trusted his judgment. And she wanted to get to know him better. Much better.

Somehow she knew that wherever he was taking her would turn out fine. And she wasn't just talking about a physical place, but a romantic one. After trusting Roarke with her life, it was easier to trust him with her feelings.

And if she was making a mistake, it wouldn't be her first. She couldn't let her disastrous past with Patrick ruin every new relationship before it had a chance to begin. She'd held Roarke's good looks and incredible charm against him for long enough to learn about his true nature. Not only was he willing to lay his life on the line for her, he'd held her so gently in the trunk when she'd mourned the loss of her father and had given her what she most needed—comfort. Now she wanted to see if he could give her more.

They'd worked well together once he'd started to open up and share his plans. But could they play together? She intended to find out.

Roarke's eyes certainly had gleamed with interest when she'd placed her hand on his knee. Oh, he'd pretended not to notice, but his voice had deepened, turning huskier, sexier. She'd wished the car didn't have bucket seats so she could have snuggled against him. But she made the most of the opportunity she had, touching him along the inside of his leg, her fingers slowly circling higher.

A muscle leaped beneath her fingers, proof positive that he was reacting to her. She liked the feel of his hard muscles beneath her hand, powerful thighs encased in slacks that reacted to her softest caress, her nails lightly teasing.

The car's headlights lit the camp, and it looked exactly as he'd described it, a large concrete garage, a raised deck with a tent already pitched, overlooking dark waters glinting under the moon.

"Why didn't the guy just build a cabin?"

"He intended to. He ran out of funds."

She didn't remove her hand from his thigh until he

switched off the engine, and then she instantly missed the contact. ''You leave the tent up?''

''I was camping here when your brother called.''

''I interrupted your vacation?'' When he nodded, she opened the car door, stood and stretched her legs. ''I'm sorry.''

''I'm not.'' He walked around the hood and took her hand. Simply by the touch of his palm he conveyed heat and safety and the promise of so much more. A beginning for both of them, together as they had not been before.

She breathed in the scent of cypress, grass and pine and ached for him to draw her into his arms, but he seemed intent on playing tour guide. When the moonlight shimmered on his face, however, she saw his eyes, hungry with need, and her mouth went dry. Anticipation hung in the air. And he'd done nothing but take her hand.

He shone a flashlight that he'd taken from the glove compartment over the water. ''That's the lake.'' He turned at a ninety-degree angle. ''And the spring's over there.''

''Is the water very cold?'' she asked, knowing she needed a shower, not just to wash, but to cool her skin, rapidly heating due to a combination of Roarke's touches, her thoughts and the private setting.

''There's one way to find out the water's temperature.'' He tugged her hand and led her not to the spring's bank, but to the platform that held his tent.

Hand-in-hand they climbed the stairs. ''Are you afraid of heights?'' he asked.

''Why?''

He led her around the tent and toward the farthest

edge. "Here's a diving perch from the platform. And the water below is deep everywhere. Jumping is the best way into the spring."

"It's that cold?"

"I prefer to think of it as...refreshing."

"Refreshing, huh? If it's that cold, maybe you could warm me up a little first."

He tugged her toward him, one hand cupping the back of her neck and twining into her hair. "What did you have in mind?"

At his suggestive tone, her heart skipped and skidded. She leaned into him and wrapped her arms around his neck, pressed her chest against his, breathed in his masculine scent. Her breasts ached for his touch, her knees seemed to have gone boneless and her breaths came in gulps. "How about a kiss?"

"Whatever the lady wants," he leaned until his mouth just touched hers, "the lady gets."

She didn't know which of them would close the last remaining gap. She only knew his breath made her skipping heartbeat start to sprint. It seemed as if she'd been waiting all day for this kiss, and now that it was almost here, she wasn't ready. Wasn't ready to feel this overwhelming need. Wasn't ready for the multitude of sensations that caused her to want to explore every inch of him. Wasn't ready to feel as if the entire world focused on her mouth.

From past experience, she already knew he was quite an expert in the kissing department. He kissed just like he looked—sublime. Just from one hot look, her breasts swelled and her nipples puckered. And she had a tingly warm feeling that made her pulse race.

"Damn you, kiss me already."

"Yes, ma'am."

He bit her lower lip with a taunting sensuality that left her thoughts spinning and her pulse pounding. His teasing drove her wild, and she leaned into him, enjoying his taut heat, his simmering masculinity.

"Surely you can do better than that." She meant to sound demanding. Instead, she sounded breathless. Needy. And much too eager. However, she no longer cared, craving to give in to the passion he'd kindled.

Threading her hands into his thick black hair, she tugged his head closer. Let her hips nestle against his hardness. Two could play this game.

But he smelled so good she had difficulty remembering not to try and devour him like a starving woman. Instead, she explored the shell of his ear, the muscular curve of his neck and the line of his arrogant jaw. That he was still arrogant, demanding and determined to set the pace made him all the more appealing.

His hand rested intimately on the small of her back, the other wrapped around her shoulder, cuddling her close. And still he refused to give her his mouth.

Instead, he traced a path from her brow to her cheek to her chin. She turned her head to catch his lips square on hers, and he groaned in surrender, then kissed her like a man hungry for love.

Standing so close, she could feel his hardness, knew he had to be as eager to have her as she was to have him. But he took his time, exploring her mouth with a thoroughness that kept her senses spinning. She forgot their terribly long day, the danger that would face them tomorrow, her reluctance to spend the night in a tent.

There was only now. Only Roarke. Only this compelling passion that burned between them.

His mouth claimed hers like a conquering hero, and she willingly gave him what he wanted. Then gave him more. When he eased his mouth from hers, she gulped air, trying to catch a breath, trying to rein in her emotions, trying to gather her wits about her.

He didn't give her the chance. "You did say you wanted a bath?"

"A bath?" She could barely think through the heat he'd fired up inside her.

"You *can* swim?" he asked softly, a hint of mischievousness in his tone as he took off his shoes and placed the contents of his pockets on the floor.

She nodded, and suddenly her head cleared. He'd eased her out onto the diving platform that overlooked the spring. Oak branches sheltered them in a cocoon of magic as moonlight filtered through and glinted off the opal-black waters below.

"Let's jump."

"But—"

He barely gave her time to kick off her shoes before he tugged her to the edge of the platform and yanked her with him into the air. She fell and the wind rushed through her hair. Instinctively, she held her breath. They struck the water with a splash.

The water, much colder than she'd expected, saturated her clothes, and she started kicking even as she still plunged downward. She reached the surface, laughing and relaxed, the fire he'd started earlier keeping away the chill from the cold waters.

With a smile in her heart, she flung her hair out of her eyes and searched for Roarke, who suddenly came up right beside her. She licked a water droplet off her lip, deliberately suggestive. "You didn't give me time to take off my clothes."

"If I had, you wouldn't be swimming right now," he stated with a husky urgency that left no doubt in her mind how much he wanted to make love.

She treaded water, slowly becoming accustomed to the cool temperature of the spring. Not ten feet away from where they swam, she saw a flat rock jutting from the bank. While her clothes needed washing, she didn't want to wear them, as their weight dragged her down.

She swam toward the spit of rock and found a shallow place to stand where she could remove her clothes and throw them onto the rock. Roarke followed her and then tried to take her into his arms. Playful, she ducked under the surface, but didn't make a clean getaway. He grabbed her ankle and pulled her back.

Laughing, she surfaced to find herself barely able to take a breath before he dunked her. She went with his strength and discovered that while the water here was above her head, he could stand. But not for long. She grabbed his ankles and tugged; she toppled him, and then they both came up sputtering for air.

Alexandra spat water into an arc and floated on her back, gazing up at the stars. With the city lights miles away, she could pick out the constellation Orion by the bright three stars that represented the hunter's belt and the planet Venus, easily the brightest object in the sky after the moon.

Beside her Roarke also floated, his dark hair slicked back from his handsome face, his inch-long lashes spiked with droplets of water. In the moonlight, his face appeared all dark planes and mysterious angles, his eyes reflected a moonbeam, their shadows steeped in sensuality.

He swept her into his arms, capturing her as easily as a pirate on the high seas. His powerful arms closed around her shoulder and under her legs and he carried her toward the shore with little visible effort.

"I don't want you to catch cold." He spoke with a gentle huskiness that rekindled the blaze he'd started with the kiss that had fired her soul.

Naked in his arms, yet perfectly relaxed except for the fire burning in her belly, she gazed up at him, wondering how she'd gotten so lucky as to be in Roarke's arms. He wasn't just drop-dead gorgeous, he was kind and sensitive and gentle. And as she recalled his playful antics in the water she remembered that beneath those wet pants he had the sexiest, tightest, cutest butt she'd ever seen.

"I'm plenty warm," she murmured truthfully.

Her limbs seemed to generate a sustaining heat all their own. Everywhere he touched her, he shot fire into her flesh. It was an exciting feeling, the cool water flowing over her heated skin, her hair floating along the surface, her cheek pressed to his massive chest, her ear picking up the rapid beat of his heart.

She expected him to set her down once they reached the bank. But Roarke carried her up two flights of steps, straight to his tent. It was dark inside, and she couldn't see much.

When he finally set her back on her feet, her bare toes cuddled into a thick carpet. "Don't move."

She heard him removing his clothes. He had picked up his wallet and now he was rummaging through it.

She heard the sound of paper tearing. A match flared, and she could see him lighting a lantern. She got her first eyeful of Roarke in the nude, and the sight stole her breath. He was absolutely, spectacularly, amazingly stunning. In the orange glow of the lantern's light, his wet skin shimmered with bronze highlights, defining his remarkably muscular shoulders and massive chest which decreased to a tapered waist. When he straightened and advanced toward her, the light silhouetted his body, and she glimpsed evidence of his arousal, already sheathed in a condom.

She took satisfaction in the fact that he obviously wanted her as much as she wanted him, took satisfaction in the fact that he practiced safe sex, took satisfaction in the fact that she felt so comfortable with this man who'd been a stranger only a couple of days ago. He closed the distance between them before she took in much more of their surroundings, and suddenly she realized that while she'd been staring at him, she'd been standing there bathed in the lantern's revealing light.

"See anything you like?" she asked, slightly uncomfortable with her nudity but unwilling to admit it—especially around a man so perfect and extraordinarily good-looking that he probably never had one doubt about his own appearance. Frolicking in the water was one thing, standing before him in the light naked was another.

"You're a feast for a starving man, and I'm just deciding where to start tasting you."

She swallowed hard.

He came close enough for her to feel the heat radiating off his body, but not so close that he touched her. The anticipation was sweet torture that made her blood thrum in her ears and her heart swell with unaccustomed yearnings.

"I *was* going to dry you with a towel," he whispered, "but I'm rather thirsty," he paused, leaned over and delicately licked her throat, "so I think I'll just use my tongue."

As she shivered slightly, he licked the tip of one breast, and she let out a tiny moan from the back of her throat.

She wanted more, much more. Yet he seemed determined to draw out their pleasure. Slowly, sensuously, he explored every inch of her: her breasts, her belly, her thighs, parting her legs to taste her core, leaving no part untouched until she drew so tight she thought she'd explode. Throwing her head back, she released a primal shout, her hands gripping his shoulders as he held her on the edge.

And when she couldn't take one more caress, one more sensuous stroke, he led her to an air mattress covered with clean-smelling sheets and soft blankets on the tent's floor. Grateful that she need no longer force her legs to stand while she felt so weak, she yanked him down, fused her mouth to his and demanded with every inch of her that he finish what he'd started.

"I'm sorry," he murmured.

"For…what?"

"I can't wait any longer." He sheathed himself inside her with one smooth movement.

More than ready, she wrapped her legs around him, reveling in sheer pleasure. And then she couldn't form another coherent thought. There was only Roarke, his arms around her, his hard body thrusting into her.

Her breath came in gasps. His hands held her head, and his mouth melded with hers. He took her higher, harder and then ignited the passion sparking inside her until she exploded into a single white-hot flame.

As her breathing slowed and he continued to hold her, her brain slowly re-engaged. She thought she'd heard him shout her name when he'd peaked, but she couldn't be sure. She thought he'd lost himself there at the end, but she couldn't be sure of that either. In fact, the only thing she was sure about was that they were good together. Very, very good.

And it wasn't just the sex. Even now he held her tenderly, almost reverently. The heat in his eyes had mellowed but hadn't been extinguished. She hoped it would never go out. She liked the idea of Mr. Perfect needing her, wanting her so badly that he'd actually lost some of his perfect control. She liked that he'd been so wild for her that he couldn't hold back.

And she felt so good that she didn't want to talk, didn't want to risk spoiling the most perfect night of her life. So as he shifted to her side, she cuddled against him and let him pull a sheet over both of them, ready to sleep in his arms.

Even spent, she couldn't totally relax. The passion had been too strong, too wondrous to let her go. It felt good, and right, to pillow her head on him, breathe in his scent, twine her feet with his. She realized then that she never again wanted to sleep alone.

Twice during the night, they wakened and made love. And each time was more wonderful and exciting than the last, as they learned how to please one another. She explored his body as he had hers, learning that she held an awesome power over this man. A power she vowed to use wisely. She knew he was still healing, and despite his air of invincibility, she knew he was vulnerable.

However, she recognized that ever since the first moment they'd met, a special attraction, a chemistry, a heightened awareness, had sizzled between them. Taking things to the next level, making love, hadn't extinguished the flames but seemed to have fueled them. She couldn't get enough of this man and he seemed to return her ardor.

Happy and content, she fell asleep in the early morning hours.

ALEXANDRA AWAKENED late the next morning to the scent of sizzling bacon and frying eggs. Sitting up, she took her first good look around the tent. The mattress lay on a thick-piled rug. A nightstand with books and an electric lamp sat next to the bed. She grinned when she realized that his tent had electricity, but he'd lit the lantern last night for atmosphere. She had suspected he was a romantic at heart, and now she knew for sure.

Thoughtful, Roarke had left her a bathrobe, and she slipped into it, perusing his bookcase, curious to learn his tastes. The variety didn't surprise her. Next to Clancy, Ludlum and Grisham she saw books about foreign countries, another on defusing bombs, several mysteries, a few comic books and even a Harry Potter. He had well-thumbed magazines running the gamut from *Mercenary Men* to *Playboy* to *Surfing the Net*.

On his nightstand was a picture of a younger Roarke

with his arm around a smiling young woman. Surrounding the happy-faced couple, a herd of giraffes gathered, one of them biting Roarke's straw hat. Alexandra knotted the belt on the robe and picked up the picture to examine it more closely. The blond-haired woman, Sydney, she presumed, was extremely thin, pretty, and fragile-looking. She possessed a certain vivaciousness and a warmth to her smile that Alexandra found appealing.

Roarke strode in and Alexandra did nothing to hide her interest in the picture. "You both looked so happy here."

"It was taken the week before she died." Roarke spoke without any apparent pain, but she could see from the shadows in his eyes that he remained haunted by her death.

Alexandra put the picture back, carefully positioning it exactly where she'd found it. She didn't want to trample on his grief. And she refused to be jealous of a woman who'd passed on. "Is that breakfast? I'm starving."

As if agreeing to drop any serious matters, Roarke held open the tent flap for her. "Let's go eat."

As she exited the tent and was greeted by bright sunshine filtering through the shading limbs of giant oaks, she felt none of the embarrassment she might have expected after making love with Roarke for the first time. At peace, she let her contentment from last night flow through her. Her body was satiated, her mind at peace.

Even if Roarke *ever* suggested making their relationship more permanent, she could see no future in it. While she eventually wanted to marry and have kids, she couldn't picture herself with a man who was away more than he was home. Or with someone who risked his life on a daily basis. So why was she falling for a guy who could leave her in fear every morning that he might not come home that night?

He wasn't right for her. Yet despite every rational thought to the contrary, somehow, she'd fallen in bed with him. And she didn't know if she'd made a mistake or simply needed more time with him to establish whether or not what they had together was simply lust or real love.

Roarke had a table and chairs set up on the deck overlooking the spring. He'd plugged a portable stove into an electric outlet and had cooked fried eggs, crisp bacon and set out a pitcher of orange juice.

She placed a napkin on her lap. "I wish we could stay a week."

Roarke looked pleased as he passed her a platter of bacon. "I thought you didn't like camping?"

"I like camping with you," she told him.

His eyes flared. "And I like being inside you."

"We were good together, weren't we?"

At her comment, the heat in his eyes blazed. Her stomach fluttered.

She would never have chosen this man to love, but choice didn't seem to have much to do with her lusty response to him. Even in a T-shirt and boxer shorts he looked impossibly yummy, his tanned muscles catching sunlight and reminding her of both his inner and outer strength.

She poured some orange juice, her hands trembling slightly as she recalled the things they'd done together and the passions he'd stirred inside her. If their attraction was only lust, three times should have more than satisfied her. But as she sat across from him, she wondered if she'd ever get enough. Was she really feeling love?

Perhaps. She couldn't be sure.

As strong as her growing feelings were about him, she needed time to accept that she loved him. Time to reevaluate the kind of man she wanted. Time to see if they could both change enough to fit into one another's lives. Time to let life go on and to see if these feelings remained. And the only way to do that was to bring the conversation back to more mundane topics.

"If I didn't have my building under construction, I'd be content to camp for a few days."

"Only a few days?"

"Maybe a week," she conceded, looking up and letting him see the desire in her eyes. "But I do have a skyscraper to finish."

He arched an arrogant brow. "You'd leave paradise and me for steel and concrete?"

"I'm a greedy woman. I don't see why I can't have both."

Chapter Twelve

Roarke made love to Alexandra one more time before he let her call her engineer. And all the while she spoke on the phone, he castigated himself. A man who was responsible for a woman's life had no business being distracted by her femininity. When danger could come from any direction, Roarke needed to be thinking about tactics, assessing their position. His fantasizing about making love could get her killed. Floored by his own behavior with Alexandra over the past twelve hours, knowing he should never have touched a client, never mind made love to her, he tried to justify his behavior to himself.

Although he'd let down his guard, he'd done so in a very safe place, and he didn't regret the wonderful interlude. He'd found Alexandra just as passionate in bed as she was about how she lived her life. And he believed she wouldn't have responded to him as she had unless she felt something in return.

Both of them were cautious. Both had been hurt before and neither was ready for the irresistible passion that arced between them. She wasn't the first woman he'd made love to since Sydney had died, but she was the first woman he'd brought to his camp and who had slept the entire night in his bed. That he liked Alexandra so much had made him try to resist his growing attraction to her. He sensed she wasn't a woman who gave in to passion lightly.

He simply couldn't resist what she'd so freely offered. And now that he knew her better, now that he'd held her in his arms, he was more determined than ever to keep her safe.

Her face grim, Alexandra rejoined him on the deck after making her phone call to her engineer. Her fingers shook, her voice was tight. "I've got to go to the site today."

"What happened?"

"Someone set off an explosion."

"Was anyone hurt?"

She shook her head, her eyes bleak. "But the city inspectors have questions that only I can answer. No further work can be done until decisions are made. I have to be there."

"You realize that whoever is after you may have sabotaged your project to make you come out of hiding?"

She took his hand and her eyes locked with his. "Please, Roarke. I have to be there today."

Although he might have tried to protect Alexandra by hiding out, her disappearance wouldn't solve the problem—not long-term—and not as long as someone wanted those papers. He had to discover who was after her and why. Until he did, she wouldn't be safe.

Now that he knew the construction site was being watched, he just might be able to catch the watchers. Fairly certain he could disguise Alexandra so even her own mother wouldn't recognize her from two feet away, he felt confident he could protect her.

A half hour later, Roarke pulled the car into a shopping center, and while Alexandra bought them clothes with cash, he purchased actors' makeup, wigs and non-prescription contact lenses that would disguise eye color. Roarke traded in the vehicle for another at a used-car lot and then drove straight to a hotel.

In the privacy of the hotel room, he and Alexandra changed their clothes. He instructed her to tie up her hair and then he went to work on her skin, turning her olive skin to a dark mahogany. A wig of dreads and brown contact lenses completed her transformation into an African-American woman. A double-D bra, the cups stuffed with tissues, completed her outfit.

Although neatly dressed for business, Alexandra stared at herself in the mirror with a frown. "A business woman wouldn't wear dreads."

He frowned at her, knowing she was right. "What do you suggest? You want to change the clothes and go as a mechanic? I have an extra uniform." He pointed to the shopping bag, then the uniform he'd bought for himself. "It's comfy."

"Yeah, but I want to discuss business with the city inspectors. I don't think a janitor's uniform will do the trick." Alexandra reached up and donned the wig that simulated an Afro haircut. "With a hard hat, this might work."

Roarke had changed his own appearance by making himself look like a nerd in a janitor's uniform. He now wore contacts to make his blue eyes brown, horn-rimmed glasses taped at the nose piece and a blond wig that he greased down so the hair looked dirty and matted.

Slouching his shoulders, he turned to face Alexandra. "What do you think?"

She rolled up his old shirt and tucked it under the elastic at the waistband of his pants, giving him a pot belly. "That's better. So what's the plan?"

"We drive onto the construction site like we own the place."

"Have you forgotten the security guard at the gate? He won't let us past if he doesn't recognize me."

"Does the guard know your voice?"

"I don't know."

Roarke pointed to the hotel phone. "Call him now, tell him you've hired a woman to take your place. Then describe what you look like now. When we arrive, he should wave us through."

She gave him a grin, and her white teeth gleamed against her mahogany skin. "You're sneaky."

"Let's hope I'm sneaky enough to catch the bad guys in the act. While you're working, I'll be hunting for them."

She cocked her head to the side. "Won't that be dangerous?"

Roarke handed her the phone, thinking how beautiful she looked, but then he'd think she looked good if her skin were green, purple or blue. "Make your phone call and let's head out. I'll phone Carleton and ask him to stay with you once we get to the site."

"You're leaving?" she asked.

"I want you protected while I look around. I suspect Top Dog or more of his men will be watching the site."

A half hour later, the guard at the gate waved them through with no hassles. Carleton remained next to Alexandra while she strode over to Aaron Blake, her engineer, and whispered her identity in his ear. The man tried not to stare at her, then calmly took her elbow and guided her toward the city inspectors who'd converged around the newly poured concrete where the explosion had done the most damage.

Roarke merged into the shadows and let his eyes slowly adjust to the bright sunshine. He peered at the area, deciding from where he would watch the site if he had drawn that assignment.

A boat fished along the river, but kept moving along on the outgoing tide. At least he didn't have to search the waterfront and that narrowed his options.

On either side of the construction site, the view would be blocked. The best observing would be done from the offices across the street. Roarke took out a pair of binoculars and one by one studied the buildings, paying careful attention to rooms that appeared vacant, those without curtains or blinds, those with empty balconies that lacked furniture. He spied several and memorized their floor and placement before heading across the street.

Although he didn't like leaving Alexandra's side, even with Carleton there to protect her, Roarke needed to end this constant threat to her safety. They needed more clues to go on than the fingerprints of a man supposed to have been dead for over twenty-five years. While he knew Carleton had continued to dig for more clues, Roarke suspected he would find nothing more. The dead man had disappeared too long ago and had likely covered his tracks well.

As Roarke headed toward the gate and the building across the street, he turned back to see Alexandra, Aaron and Carleton walking with her coworkers toward an exterior elevator that would take them to the fifth story where a second explosion had taken place.

Around him, work continued as usual. Concrete trucks rumbled through the gate, backhoes and loaders worked in tandem to level the parking area, while men in hard hats scampered nimbly over scaffolding, directing cranes that lifted and deposited steel I-beams on the top levels.

Again Roarke took out a pair of binoculars and from a side angle checked the offices across the street. A telescope peeking through a gauze curtain caught his eye.

Gotcha!

Unless the local cops had a stakeout across the street, Roarke had almost assuredly found Top Dog or more of his cell. Suspicions heightened further by a sudden curtain movement, Roarke counted floors and headed directly to the suspicious-looking office.

He crossed the street, entered the insurance building and pressed the elevator button for the seventh floor. He counted offices, beginning at the end of the hallway, withdrew his gun, checked it, reholstered the weapon in his ankle holster and then knocked softly on the door.

"What do you want?" someone yelled from the interior.

"It's maintenance," Roarke replied, slurring his words a little. "The AC is out in this section."

"The air's fine, bud."

Roarke knew men on a stakeout weren't supposed

to open the door to strangers. He also knew that agents frequently broke the rules—especially agents that didn't want to sit 24/7 in a stiflingly hot room with a broken air conditioner.

"Hey, it's no sweat off my back if you don't want me to check the wiring. If you see smoke, just call 911," Roarke bluffed and waited, every muscle tense.

He could have guessed wrong. This might not be the right office. Or the man in there could be legit. But he removed his gun from its holster and aimed it at the door, sensing trouble on the other side.

When no one came to open the door, Roarke removed a few sharp tools from his pocket to pick the lock. Every agent learned the basics, but he hadn't practiced this skill in years. Unfortunately, picking a lock wasn't like riding a bike—he'd forgotten that it was much harder than it looked in the movies. Sweaty fingers and nerves that sang a song telling him time was of the essence made him fumble. Finally, he heard the telltale click and eased open the door.

Roarke silently and slowly slipped into the room, his gun held before him. The foyer was a straight shot to the office area where a man stood with his back to Roarke.

The gauze curtain fluttered. And Roarke's heart turned to ice. Hidden behind the curtain was a sniper's rifle and scope.

Knowing he had only seconds to make a decision before the man pulled the trigger, Roarke spoke slowly, needing to make sure before he took action that this guy wasn't from a legitimate government agency. "Are you with SWAT?"

Roarke had hoped the man would turn from the

window and lose his aim across the street. As tense seconds passed, Roarke realized, a cop would have identified himself by now. If this were a legitimate operation, this man would have politely ushered him out. He damn well wouldn't ignore him.

Instead of turning to face him, the cool-headed sniper pulled the trigger, firing a shot into the construction site across the street. Then in one smooth motion, the sniper pivoted, aiming the rifle at Roarke.

Knowing seconds could make the difference between living and dying, Roarke dived and rolled, firing his gun as shots whizzed by his body and embedded themselves into drywall. Roarke's first wild shots missed.

The sniper threw down his rifle and pulled out a revolver. Without one second of hesitation, Roarke rolled again and fired.

Roarke took out the sniper with his sixth shot. In five seconds it was all over. Roarke felt no satisfaction. He'd shot instinctively, his aim true and the man was now dead. And a dead man couldn't tell him who he worked for.

Nothing had turned out as he'd planned. At least all the guns had had silencers so none of the people working in the building would be alarmed.

But Roarke knew he'd made a mistake. He'd wanted to take the man alive. Now he'd lost the opportunity to seek the answers he needed. And he couldn't stay and take the heat for this mess with the local authorities. Although this fight had been self defense he could lose his license if he left the scene. Yet he had to get back to Alexandra.

Before he'd climbed back to his feet, Roarke heard a horrible crash from across the street.

He raced to the window and fear pierced him. The crane operator had lost control and a deadly I-beam had swung into the building. Roarke saw a body fall four stories off the roof. He didn't stay to see more details.

To hell with his license. Alexandra needed him. He just prayed she'd still be alive when he finally got to her.

Roarke ran full out across the street without bothering to reholster his weapon. While he suspected the sniper's shot had caused the crane accident, he couldn't be sure there wouldn't be another of Top Dog's men on the site, a foe who could reach Alexandra before he could.

Roarke dodged traffic, pedestrians and a hot-dog cart. He rushed past the gate. Heard sirens in the distance. He ignored screams from passersby, the choking dust, and the shouting confusion of construction workers. It brought back vivid memories of the bombing of an American embassy and another woman's death.

Alexandra and Carleton had been heading to the roof. Was she up there when the I-beam crashed? He shuddered at the thought of hundreds of pounds of falling steel slicing through flesh, flattening the scaffolding, rocketing like a bullet between floors. Would he recognize their bodies if he found them? Ruthlessly, he shoved the grisly thought away. He was not going to lose Alexandra or his friend.

Roarke skidded to a halt at the base of the building and tilted his head back to look up. The building reminded him of one he'd built out of Popsicle sticks as a kid. Except the sticks were steel I-beams and looked ready to fall.

The elevator cage looked stuck between two floors and dangled at an angle by one cable. Roarke squinted through the dust, trying to make out Alexandra's blue dress or Carleton's khaki slacks. He thought he might have caught a glimpse of them, but he couldn't be sure.

One thing he did know. They were up there somewhere and he was damn well going to find them.

Roarke flagged over a loader and directed the man to lower the bucket. He climbed in and shouted over the engine. "Get me up there."

The loader operator nodded and boosted Roarke to the second story. From there, he was on his own. The damage on this level was bad, and he knew the farther he climbed, the worse the structural damage would be.

Roarke gritted his teeth, found a ladder and climbed to the third story. Three people were trapped inside the elevator. Was Alexandra one of them? His heart pumped with fear. A three-story fall would likely kill everyone trapped inside.

From here he could see the elevator cage clearly. Carleton was sitting slumped on the floor. And Alexandra! She was there, too, with another woman, but he felt no relief. While Alexandra was still alive, she was in too much danger for him to feel anything but more panic.

"Alexandra! You hurt?"

"Bumps and bruises. But Carleton took a knock on his head. He's breathing and conscious but too dizzy to stand. You have to get us out of here before the cable breaks."

The machines below couldn't reach this high. From here, he could see that the crane operator had been shot by the sniper, and even if Roarke could climb down and then up into the crane's cab before the elevator fell, Roarke didn't know how to operate the machine.

"Any suggestions?" Roarke asked, knowing she was much more familiar with the building than he.

"Can you get to the top floor?" she asked.

"Maybe, why?"

"There's extra line up there we use for securing the scaffolding. If you could toss us a rope, we could climb down."

Leave it to Alexandra to figure out a way to rescue herself. He just hoped her idea would work. Roarke edged away from the elevator, placing his feet carefully before looking up.

Climbing to the next story wouldn't be easy. He considered going back for the ladder, pulling it up behind him and using it again when he spied a huge hole in the roof and a pile of supplies under it. Could the lines Alexandra had spoken about have fallen through the broken area?

This time, luck was with him. He found the rope with no trouble, heaved it over his shoulder and hurried back to the building's edge. "I've got it."

"Good, the wind's picking up," Alexandra's voice remained firm, but he could still hear her nervousness. When he looked out to the dangling elevator, he could see more reason for concern. The damaged cage swayed back and forth. The other woman huddled in the corner, clinging to Carleton with one hand and the cage with the other. If the cage collided with the building, the cable might snap from the force.

Roarke uncoiled the rope. "Alexandra, you're going to have to open the cage door so you can catch the rope."

"Okay." She slid the door open and he could see all three people much better. The two women had strapped Carleton to the cage with his belt. Alexandra now held onto the cage with one hand and onto the other woman with the other. She leaned out of the swaying cage, depending on the other woman to keep her from falling.

As the cage careened in his direction, Roarke tossed the rope. The cage turned, the opening no longer facing him and Alexandra missed.

"Steady," she told him. "We'll get it next time."

Roarke reeled the rope back in and readied himself for another try. He'd been in some tight spots in his life, but he'd never been so nervous.

He tried again. This time the cage door faced the right direction.

But his throw was too low.

"Almost," Alexandra told him as he grimly reeled in the line again.

The next time, his throw was perfect. Alexandra grabbed the rope and the people below let out a cheer. Roarke hadn't even realized they had an audience.

"Tie off your end to the cage and I'll drop my end to the ground," he instructed Alexandra.

She worked quickly and Roarke tossed the line down to one of the construction crew.

"Don't hold it too tight or it'll put too much pressure on the cable," Alexandra told them.

And then while Roarke held his breath, Alexandra insisted that the other woman climb down first.

The woman was frightened but determined. Roarke told her how to wrap the rope around her legs, so she wouldn't have to hold all her weight with her arms. Right after the woman started down the line, Carleton insisted that Alexandra go next. Roarke's friend had revived enough from the bump on his head to climb down by himself.

As Alexandra slid down the line, Roarke climbed down from the third to the second story, staying level with her, shouting encouragement. When he reached the second story, the loader operator lifted up his bucket for Roarke. He climbed in and rode the bucket to the ground. Heart battering his ribs, pulse pounding, he shoved his way into the crowd to gather Alexandra safely into his arms.

"Hold me tight," he whispered in her ear.

Her eyes widened in surprise. "You're shaking."

Roarke pulled her away from underneath the dangling elevator cage. "I've never been so frightened in my life. If something had happened to you..." He paused as his throat clogged with emotion, "I never would have forgiven myself."

Carleton joined them a moment later. Clearly he'd overheard Roarke's words and grinned. Roarke clapped him on the shoulder without releasing Alexandra from his embrace. "You okay?"

Carleton nodded. "Good thing I have a hard head."

Roarke frowned. "Sorry. My fault."

Alexandra pulled back from Roarke's embrace, puzzlement in her eyes. "You can't blame yourself for an accident."

"You don't understand. The I-beam dropped when the crane operator was shot by a sniper from across the street."

"Sniper? Shots?" Obviously stunned, Alexandra rocked back on her heels. "I didn't hear any shots. I thought he'd had a heart attack or something. That poor man!"

She peered over Roarke's shoulder at the dead crane operator, her face reflecting her sadness, her shoulders shuddering. Construction workers hadn't moved the body, leaving the crime scene untouched for the homicide detectives. Another body lay unmoving on the ground, the neck twisted. Alexandra looked into Roarke's face and must have read some of the guilt he felt. "It's not your fault."

"If I'd moved more quickly, the sniper wouldn't have made that shot."

"What do you mean?"

As he explained what had happened, he escorted Alexandra to their vehicle. Staying to answer the police questions would just make protecting her all the harder. With the Agency's close ties to local law enforcement, he needed to escort her away quickly before the police detained them. Carleton volunteered to stay behind and answer the police's questions.

Roarke and Alexandra stopped in the construction trailer's office and grabbed the extra set of documents still hidden inside the cardboard blueprint tube, because Roarke had no intention of coming back to this construction site again—not until Top Dog was dead or behind bars. He didn't care if they blew up the entire building—he wouldn't allow Alexandra to risk her life again.

Once they reached their parked car, they overheard Carleton talking to a foreman, claiming he didn't need medical treatment, and that the bang on his head had just stunned him but done no permanent damage.

Roarke drove out the gate without problems. Beside him, Alexandra took tissues and the special cream he'd bought and removed the dark makeup from her skin. One box of tissues later and she looked normal. He had her carefully gather all the tissues and the wig into a trash bag, and then they dumped it in a city waste receptacle.

Alexandra hadn't said much since he'd told her what he'd found across the street. He suspected while she might be bothered by the fact that he'd been forced to kill a man, she was more upset over the innocent crane operator's death. To her credit, she hadn't said one word about the destruction of her building, a catastrophe that would put her weeks behind schedule.

"I can't let anyone else die," she murmured. "We have to put a stop to this. That crane operator probably had a wife, kids. The construction worker who fell couldn't be older than twenty-five."

"I'm sorry." He could tell from her tone as well as from her demeanor that she was torn. She didn't slouch in defeat or lower her head, but stared straight ahead. He could tell she'd come to some kind of decision.

"Being sorry won't bring them back. It won't put food on the table. It was one thing to take risks when it was my life, but when perfectly innocent people are shot..." She let out a long, low sigh. "I've had enough, Roarke. Take me home."

"Home?"

"To my apartment."

"That's not a good idea. The Agency had men watching your construction site. They'll have men watching your apartment, too."

"That's what I'm counting on." She must have seen the doubt on his face. "You can drop me off on the corner and keep going. This is my problem and I'm going to solve it my own way."

"You think I'd abandon you?" That she would even consider the possibility of him leaving her to face this alone made him realize that although they'd shared an incredible night of lovemaking, too many important things hadn't been said between them.

"You have too much integrity to quit on me, so I'm firing you."

"You can't fire me."

"I just did."

"I told you before. You can't fire me because you didn't hire me. And until I hear from your brother, I'm sticking to you like glue."

"I mean it, I'm not going to have one more person die over those papers."

At least she hadn't tried to fire him again. Instead she'd used a different negotiating tactic, coming at the problem from another angle. While he admired her determination to take matters into her own hands, he was tired of tamping down his temper. He was more than annoyed that she wanted to be rid of him, and furious that she thought she could face down these men on her own.

But Roarke was not a man to allow his temper to show—unless it suited his purpose. Now was not the time. Alexandra had just been through a harrowing experience. Most women would have wanted *more* protection. Yet Alexandra wanted him to just up and disappear.

And then there was the guilt factor. One he recognized all too well. Although she hadn't pulled the trigger, she felt guilty over the crane operator's death.

But getting herself killed wouldn't bring the man back to life. However, even if she wanted to sacrifice herself, Roarke wouldn't allow it. He wouldn't let any client make such an irrational decision, and he especially wouldn't let a woman he cared about as much as he did Alexandra just walk into a trap and give herself up to the enemy.

As these thoughts raced through his mind, he knew he'd resort to force if it meant keeping her safe. He'd much prefer to reason with her, convince her to do things his way. Past experience with Alexandra had taught him she could be reasonable, so Roarke reined in his temper and parked downtown across the street from Jacksonville's Riverwalk.

A boardwalk dotted with shops and restaurants lined the St. John's River. Tourists and natives strolled along, eating ice cream, pushing baby strollers and wandering through the stores.

"What are we doing here?" Alexandra asked him, not even bothering to get out of the car.

"Taking a moment—"

"I don't need a moment. I've decided—"

"You?"

"They're *my* papers. It's *my life at risk. My* building that was ruined. *My* crane operator that's dead. It's *my* decision." She took a deep breath and let the air out in a rush. "I know you want to take over. That it's your nature to take over—but this is my problem."

"*Our* problem," he corrected her, his tone gentle, but she must have heard his steely resolve and a hint of his anger, because she squared her shoulders and lifted her chin, her eyes defiant, ready to do battle.

"We've done things your way. And it hasn't worked out."

"You're still alive," he pointed out, crossing his arms over his chest and reminding himself that she was upset. She was only trying to dump him because she felt guilty. Her decision had nothing to do with him personally. So why did he feel so bruised? Why did he feel as if he'd let her down?

"I'm alive, but I can't work. I can't visit my friends or see my family. I can't go back to my apartment, and we just ran away from the police back there."

"So what do you want to do?"

"Give the bad guys what they want."

"You want me to hand you over to them?"

"I don't want *you* to do anything." She drew herself up straight. "*I'm* going to give them the papers that my brother sent me."

Chapter Thirteen

Ever since Alexandra had seen the crane operator's lifeless body and the fear in the eyes of the inspectors who could have died, too, she'd known she couldn't let the situation go on. No more lives would be lost over those papers Jake had sent her. Right now she wished she'd never received them. Then she'd never have been involved.

She knew Roarke disagreed with her conclusion, but, she had to give him credit, he'd heard her out calmly. "Whatever twenty-five-year-old secret is in those papers can stay a secret. It's not worth any more lives."

Roarke gripped the car's steering wheel loosely, his emotions contained and controlled, his tone reasonable, although she suspected he was annoyed with her. "And how do you suggest making a deal? We don't know who is after you."

"I don't need to know." Alexandra leaned back in the car seat, but she couldn't relax. Not with both sets of papers in the car—one set in the blueprint tube, the other copy packed with her clothes. "You said they'll be watching my apartment?"

"Yes?"

She'd worked out a simple plan that shouldn't endanger anyone. "So we'll turn on the light outside my front door, and leave one set of papers on my front stoop. If they want them, they'll come and get them."

She glanced over at him, waiting for him to poke holes in her strategy, waiting for him to tell her why she shouldn't hand over the documents.

But Roarke said nothing.

His face gave away none of his thoughts.

While she wondered what was going on in his mind, she wasn't going to let him convince her to go on as they had been. She wanted her life back. And even if her biological father had been murdered over the secrets in those papers, she wasn't about to give her life for them, too.

If that made her a coward, so be it. She wouldn't have more lives on her conscience, not while she believed she could put a stop to the plotting and spying and killing. Maybe Roarke was accustomed to living in this kind of world—she wasn't. She wanted to go home to the same place every night, sleep in the same bed. And if Roarke condemned her for ending his assignment, she would live with that, too.

Roarke spotted a pay phone nearby. "Wait here. I want to call Carleton, make sure the police didn't hassle him and he got back to the office okay, see if he's all right and if he's found anything new."

"Okay. But I'm not changing my mind."

Apparently Roarke knew better than to argue with her. He didn't even try. She was just happy not to have more disagreements between them.

Despite her earlier words, she was grateful that

Roarke refused to abandon her. Her enemies were pros. She knew she wasn't equipped to deal with them. She also knew that after she gave up the papers, the bald-headed man Roarke called Top Dog might want to tie up all the loose ends by killing her. Since Roarke hadn't tried to deter her by pointing out that possibility, she felt as if he agreed that the benefits of her plan exceeded the risks.

He made several phone calls, returned to the car and slid behind the wheel. "Harrison still hasn't heard from your brother. And my license won't be suspended although the police want to talk with me after this assignment is over."

"And Carleton?"

"He's fine. He's got an ice pack on his head, but his computer search for Top Dog has turned up nothing new. The CIA is notoriously close-mouthed about their classified operations. His sources within the agency don't go back that many years."

"Do the FBI and CIA spy on each other?"

"We work together. We share information. And sometimes we investigate one another when our jurisdictions overlap."

"Who was your third call to?" she asked curiously.

"Law enforcement." When she didn't say anything more, he added. "There's a job I needed to set up."

The way he oh-so-casually mentioned other work made her think that he believed she wouldn't need his protection much longer. She certainly hoped so. And yet she would miss his company. If she had to run from strangers, she couldn't have had a better man than Roarke at her side. He had kept her alive. And he'd kept up her spirits.

She'd never resolved her feelings for him either. While she believed they had much more going for them than lust, she couldn't be sure she was in love. So she fully intended to see him again after all this trouble was over and give herself a chance to explore her feelings further.

Glancing at him sideways, she realized he'd gone into his I'm-not-talking mode. While she supposed he was angry that she'd decided to give the materials up, he hadn't said so. In fact, he hadn't said much at all, just closed off his thoughts to her.

"You're angry, aren't you?" she asked, hating the awkward silence.

"Why do you think that?"

"You've turned off the charm you ooze when you're trying to convince me to do things your way." She made the accusation, lightly, teasingly, but meant it all the same.

"Have I?"

"Don't play dumb. I know there's a brain behind that pretty face."

At her comment, he cracked a smile, a small one, but a smile nonetheless. "Let's just say I'm disappointed. But I understand why you want to give up."

"You make it sound as if I'm waving a white flag in surrender to the enemy."

He cocked one very arrogant eyebrow. "You aren't?"

"I'm winning my life back. And that's what I want—my life, not a bunch of old papers." She made her voice less confrontational. "Surely you can understand?"

"I understand. But I also understand that enemies of this country want those papers."

"We have a duplicate."

"If those papers teach terrorists to build biological weapons then our having a copy won't stop them."

"Come on. Those papers are too old to contain technology that anyone would want today."

"Maybe."

She supposed she'd have to settle for his partial agreement, although she'd hoped for a smidgen of enthusiasm. Hoped he might reach over and pat her shoulder or squeeze her hand, but he denied her that comfort, too.

Instead, he drove, swiftly and competently, back to her neighborhood. He didn't bother hiding their vehicle's approach to her apartment or their walk up the front steps, almost as if he intended to attract attention.

Unlocking her front door was unnecessary. The door opened with a simple push. She gasped as she took in the mess inside. Every drawer had been pulled out of its cabinet and emptied, her furniture slashed, the stuffing pulled out. Several large vases were broken, her closets emptied, pictures dumped on the floor. At first glance, she wondered if vandals had ransacked the place, but a closer inspection proved how methodical the search had been. No corner had gone untouched. And while some items were broken, the chaos was mostly due to a horrendous mess.

Alexandra shook her head and let out a long breath of air. *They're only things, items that can be replaced.* Her precious architectural books might be littered across the floor, but the pages hadn't been ripped out. The picture frame might be broken, but the treasured photograph of her and her parents taken when she'd been accepted to college hadn't been damaged.

As she set about clearing a path, Roarke checked the apartment for hidden intruders. But whoever had done the damage was long gone. Roarke used her phone, speaking too low for her to hear, as she replaced a winter jacket in her closet. Roarke hung up the phone and checked the locks on her windows and doors. He pulled the shades and blinds and turned on several lights.

"You're still determined?" he asked.

She nodded and gestured her arms wide to take in the apartment. "I want this over."

"Fine. Leave the mess." He placed the copy of Jake's papers, wrapped in a rubber band, on her front-door mat. "Let's get out of here."

She realized he'd tried to make the apartment look as if they were inside, but he had no intention of allowing her to stay to see if anyone accepted her offer. "Suppose someone else takes the papers?"

"That's not going to happen. I called Carleton and told him I was leaving the papers on the front stoop."

She looked at Roarke, confused. "You think Carleton is working for Top Dog?"

Roarke shook his head. "Your phone is bugged. Top Dog will have overheard my conversation with Carleton."

He sounded so confident that she didn't question him further. He took her arm and led her through the apartment to the back door.

The last time she'd fled through here, she'd been alone. Now she had Roarke, but she still worried that they might be shot at as they fled.

Roarke didn't seem overly concerned. He hadn't even drawn his weapon.

They walked out onto the terrace and around the building toward the parking garage, Alexandra holding the blueprint tube with the extra set of documents. She had an eerie sense of *déjà vu,* but the thing she found most odd was how relaxed Roarke seemed. And he wasn't faking. She knew the difference now. However, he never once let down his guard as he opened the car door for her and then slid into the driver's seat.

Puzzled, she turned to him. "I thought you said they'd be watching?"

"They are. But Top Dog will have to call the guys on stakeout with his orders. And after the confusion I caused in their operation back at the construction site, communications lines are bound to need alterations and upgrades."

Her hopes suddenly soared. "Could you have killed the man in charge?"

He shook his head. "Not likely. That man was a field agent. Orders come down from inside. Most likely Top Dog sits safely behind his title and his desk."

"Why are you so sure we aren't in much danger?" she pressed him, suddenly realizing that he hadn't told her his plans.

He casually dropped the bomb. "Because I called in backup. Remember, I told you I called law enforcement? Police have been conspicuously watching your building since before we arrived."

"What!" She dropped the blueprint tube to the floor, unable to believe he'd gone behind her back after she'd expressly made her wishes known. How dare he use the papers as bait without telling her first? How dare he risk making their enemies angrier without discussing his plans with her? How dare he betray her like that? It wasn't what he had done that made her angry, but that he hadn't bothered to tell her first.

Hurt slammed into her chest. She couldn't get past the fact that he hadn't even talked his decision over with her. He'd just gone ahead and let her think he was following her wishes, when in reality, he'd set other schemes in motion. ''Damn you. You had no right.''

''I have just as much right to follow my convictions as you do yours. That information may be invaluable.''

''You don't know that.''

''Common sense tells me that with the way these agents are trying to recover it, the info must be valuable, probably explosive.''

''But you don't work for the Agency any longer. You've compromised your obligation to your client, your obligation to me.''

''I'm sorry you see things that way.''

''You knew I would. You knew my wishes. You just didn't care—''

''I cared.''

''Not enough.'' She made a visible effort to rein in her anger. ''Besides, I thought you don't trust the police.''

''I don't.''

''Then what are they doing here?''

''Top Dog won't make a move on you if the cops are watching.'' At least he hoped Top Dog wouldn't— it all depended on how desperate his foe had gotten.

"But Top Dog can't make a move on the papers with the cops out there."

"We'll see. I'm betting he will."

Roarke pulled around the apartment complex and parked. "I think you may still get what you want." He took out his binoculars. "A cop is retrieving the papers."

"Great. Just great."

"Another man in a coat and tie just strode over, flashed ID."

"So?"

"The cop just handed the papers over to a man with a gun. He must be one of Top Dog's men."

"So now the bad guys will think I set a trap. They'll think I left the papers out there so when they retrieved them, the cops can make an arrest. They'll think I betrayed them."

Roarke shook his head, his tone filled with satisfaction. "You don't understand. Top Dog's men think they've *stolen* the papers from the cops."

"You're right. I don't understand."

"Look, if you just handed the papers to Top Dog, he'd be suspicious. This way, Top Dog thinks he stole the papers from the police. By calling in the cops, I kept you safe. The bad guys have the documents—just like you wanted."

She suddenly felt foolish for thinking that Roarke had betrayed her. But it was his own fault, damn it. He should have shared his sneaky plan with her. But, oh no, he had to go and play secret agent and scheme without her. She felt outmaneuvered and unsure of herself. The minute Roarke had failed to explain something to her, she'd believed the worst of him. She didn't trust him now and yet she'd trusted him when they'd made love.

He didn't deserve such inconsistency from her. Sure, he could have told her about the arrangements he'd made, but he'd put the performance of his job first—keeping her safe. And he'd explained after she'd asked. Was that good enough to satisfy her? She didn't know. But she felt as though she owed him an apology.

"I'm sorry."

He lowered the binoculars and replaced them in their case. He didn't pretend not to know why she'd apologized, didn't make it easy for her. "You aren't ever going to trust me, are you?"

She could have sworn ice chips floated in his ultra-blue eyes, pure coldness swimming in a pool of anger and hurt. His pain pierced her in unexpected ways. Yet all the blame wasn't hers. "Why didn't you just tell me what you'd planned?"

"I'm used to working alone. But that isn't the point," he snapped. "I'm never going to be able to tell you everything ahead of time. You want the impossible."

"But I do want you," she told him, hoping he could see she wasn't any happier about her reaction than he was. "I want to keep on seeing you after all this is over. I want to see what it's like to go out with you without looking over our shoulders. I want to see what it's like be together under normal conditions."

He stared straight ahead, not even looking at her, his voice intense, yet conversational in tone. "I'm not sure that's good enough. You aren't reacting out of stress. Someone must have hurt you…"

"His name was Patrick. He was handsome and charming and always said the right thing. We were going to marry. And then I caught him kissing another woman right in front of my office building."

"I'm not Patrick."

"I know."

"Well, guess what? I don't want a woman who can't trust."

A tense silence sizzled between them as she didn't say anything more. Was he breaking off their relationship? Was he implying he wanted nothing else to do with her? She wasn't sure. She only knew his words cut deeper that she'd have thought possible.

Had she blown her chance for a future with this man? She didn't know, didn't seem able to control her shifting emotions. She only knew that she'd never forgive herself if she didn't try to put things right. Except she was at a loss how to do so. She didn't know what to say, because words wouldn't fix the problem. Not when Roarke had pegged her so correctly.

Roarke's cell phone rang, breaking the silence and startling her. Although he kept phones in every car, he'd told her he didn't use them except in emergencies since he feared the calls could be traced.

He flipped it open, muttering, "It better be damn important for you to have called me on this line."

He listened, but instead of sharing as he once had, she heard only his side of the conversation. "Where? When? Got it."

Roarke looked over his shoulder to check and merge with the traffic, then pulled away from her apartment building. "That was Carleton. He has information for us."

ALEXANDRA WONDERED briefly if she would ever redeem herself in her own eyes. Had Patrick hurt her so badly that she was going to let it ruin her relationship with Roarke? She didn't want that to happen. And yet...

Roarke parked in front of a seafood restaurant, and they entered separately. He didn't try to take her hand, didn't so much as touch her as he opened the door for her.

Alexandra should have been hungry, but the scent of fresh-fried catfish made her stomach turn. Unable to eat while still upset by her conversation with Roarke, she took a deep breath and vowed to think of other things. When she spied Carleton sitting at a booth in the rear, his forehead bruised, she headed there. When the men ordered a meal, she asked for a cup of chicken soup and a glass of ice water.

Carleton looked from Roarke to Alexandra. Whether or not he sensed the tension between them, he didn't comment but got right down to business. "Remember the man who left fingerprints in the phone booth?"

Alexandra frowned. "The one who was supposed to have died years and years ago?"

"His name was Simon, and he once worked as an agent with your biological father."

Roarke didn't look surprised and Carleton noticed. "You'd already surmised that Alexandra's biological parents were agents, hadn't you?"

Roarke nodded.

Alexandra sipped her water. "Simon and my father were friends?"

"I don't know." Carleton passed a file to Roarke.

Big red letters stamped on the outside said Classified. "But the man who died this morning was also in that cell during one very secret assignment twenty-something years ago."

"What kind of assignment?" Roarke asked.

"That's beyond the clearance level of my source." Carleton swallowed a bite of his grouper sandwich. "It's way up there. You are dealing with someone powerful. I suggest you back off."

"I'd like to," Alexandra admitted.

Carleton took one look at the determination on Roarke's face and then shook his head. "You can't carry the weight of the world. Even your shoulders will break under the strain."

"Stop being so melodramatic and tell me what you've got," Roarke insisted. His chin might as well have been chiseled from granite.

"My source thinks it likely the documents are in code."

Alexandra's eyes widened. No wonder the writing in the diary was so boring. The words weren't meant to convey meaning. Excitement suddenly raced through her. Perhaps she and Roarke would take the extra set of documents to the FBI and have them figure out what was going on. Now that the criminals had the documents, they probably believed their secret was safe.

"But since you gave up your set of documents, I suppose we'll never solve the puzzle."

"Actually, we have another set of papers," Alexandra told Carleton.

The FBI agent didn't seem surprised. "We could take a crack at it."

Roarke shook his head. "We need someone experienced in the codes they used over twenty years ago. We have to go to the Agency."

"But—"

"It's risky," Roarke admitted, "but not as much as you'd think. The chances of us running into anyone aware of the people after us is very small. The Agency is divided into four main units: Operations, Science and Technology, Intelligence and Administration."

"It sounds complicated," Alexandra muttered.

"It is. Within Operations, there are several divisions, Covert Action, Special Operations, Counter Intelligence, Counter Terrorism and Specialized Skills. Each subunit has cells on every continent."

"Then why didn't we ask for the CIA's help in the first place?" Alexandra asked.

Roarke pushed his food away and sipped his coffee. "The people after us know that we need a cryptologist to decipher the information."

Alexandra wondered if these men ever had the pleasure of looking at any problems as clean and straightforward as architectural ones. "So they may see us coming?"

"They'll be expecting us."

Carleton ordered key lime pie for dessert. "But they won't be expecting a query from the FBI."

Roarke shook his head. "I won't let you get involved. You have children."

"I'm already involved. And those children wouldn't have been born if you hadn't saved their father."

"Can you pull off a meeting from behind the

scenes?'' Roarke asked. ''Set it up and remain anonymous?''

Carleton dabbed his mouth with a napkin. ''Sure. No problem.''

Chapter Fourteen

Roarke and Alexandra spent the night in adjoining rooms at a hotel. While Roarke wanted to crack the code and learn the secret hidden within the documents, he didn't want to risk Alexandra's life to do it. Telling himself that he owed the Agency nothing did no good. He worried about having given Top Dog the documents but hoped that Top Dog wouldn't be able to decode them either. Roarke simply couldn't turn his back on his country when he sensed that something vital to the security of the United States would be found in the documents. Nothing else could explain the effort to retrieve them after all this time.

Carleton had set up a meeting with a cryptologist, code-named Viper, through an FBI intermediary, and while everyone had used an alias, Roarke perceived that something wasn't quite right. It was almost too easy. Yet, he hadn't sensed anyone on their tail since Alexandra had left the first set of documents on her front-door mat.

Sure, the bad guys had taken the bait, but Roarke knew all too well that those kind of men didn't believe in presents dropping into their laps. They'd be suspicious and there was a chance Top Dog knew that Roarke and Alexandra possessed another set of papers.

It was almost as if the agents who'd been after them had just vanished in a puff of smoke. So why did a sense of unease keep him alert?

Was it simply Alexandra? Was he seeing danger where none existed to avoid thinking about her? Sometime during the night they'd spent at the hotel on north Jacksonville Beach, he'd admitted to himself that he'd fallen in love with her. He didn't know why, he only knew that he had thought of her as *his* ever since they'd made love.

But love might not be enough to keep them together. Roarke wasn't sure when or how, but as his feelings had grown for Alexandra, he'd gradually moved on and let go of his past. Maybe he had found closure since Sydney had died. Maybe enough time had passed for him to heal. He would always have a special place in his heart for Sydney, but he loved Alexandra with a much more mature love, a deeper love. He'd idolized Sydney and had thought her perfect. With Alexandra, he saw her faults and loved her for them.

But was love enough?

He'd like to believe so. But he knew better and the knowledge pained him. Their love would turn to bitterness and regret if Alexandra couldn't trust him. Talking about the problem wouldn't help.

He should just let her go from his life. But how could he? How could he wake up mornings and not have her smile to look forward to during the day? How could he go back in the evenings to the empty rooms of his small rental house? How could he sleep through the darkness without her curled up next to him?

This morning, he and Alexandra had eaten breakfast in the hotel dining room, like polite strangers, little discussion between them. She sported dark circles under her eyes as if she hadn't slept any better than he had. And while she'd ordered two scrambled eggs, she'd played with her food, not more than a few bites passing between her lips.

"You sure you want to come with me to meet Viper?"

"I'm sure."

"You could stay here instead." Since she'd given up her papers, Roarke hadn't spied any danger. Alexandra had given her pursuers what they wanted, and they apparently were lying low, but he wasn't taking any chances. Until he knew the contents of the documents, he couldn't be sure she was safe. Just because Top Dog had one copy didn't mean he didn't know about or want the second set.

"You trying to get rid of me?" she asked with an arch to her brow.

While he never dealt in certainties, he trusted his instincts in the field. No one was tailing them. Her apartment was no longer being watched. Nor was the construction site.

Yet the nagging feeling that something was wrong, that he'd missed something, wouldn't go away. Maybe he just couldn't believe that Alexandra's simple solution—giving the documents away—had worked. Maybe he wanted an excuse to keep her close. And maybe he should trust the instincts that had served him so well in the past.

Alexandra looked at him over the rim of her coffee cup. "I'd like to see this through."

This? Had she meant their relationship? Or had she referred to her mother's documents?

"You realize that Viper could be setting us up?"

She shrugged a delicate shoulder. "What's the worst that could happen?"

"He could steal the documents. Or tell others about them. Or he could break the code and refuse to share with us what's in them. Or he could have alerted your pursuers, who'd be waiting to kill us."

Her almond-colored eyes locked gazes with his. "You're still worried about danger? A double cross?"

"In my business, betrayal is a possibility one learns to live with."

Pain darkened her eyes. "So then how do you ever trust anyone?"

He had no answer for her question. So he winked at her and made light of the topic. "It must be my optimistic nature. I plan for every possible contingency and then expect the best to happen."

THEORETICALLY, Alexandra understood what Roarke was trying to tell her. He considered all his options and then accepted that sometimes his trust would be misplaced. While that seemed to work for him, she didn't know if she could live that way. It was too much like building a skyscraper without referring to the plans. She didn't want to wing it.

She needed a solid foundation so the walls wouldn't crumble. She couldn't reach for the sky unless each story was pinned securely on top of the last.

And yet if she didn't take a chance, she was going to lose Roarke.

She clutched the blueprint tube with the spare set of documents, her thoughts swirling as he drove them to the meeting with Viper. She paid little attention to the route from the beach back into the city; instead, she watched Roarke drive.

She liked the way his hands held the steering wheel, gently yet with absolute control, and she couldn't help recalling when those strong hands had explored her, setting her aflame with needs that had never been so strong. Last night, she'd almost walked through the connecting door between their rooms at least a dozen times.

All the talking to herself, all the hard facts that revealed that he wasn't the right man for her had failed to convince her that she shouldn't love him. She loved him from her heart because her mind hadn't yet gotten with the program. She hadn't chosen to fall in love. Love had chosen her, marked her, given her no choice. But if she didn't figure out how to build a sturdy base for their love by learning to trust again, what they had together would teeter then topple, and she'd lose him before their love had a chance to solidify.

She longed for a chance. She wanted to grow old with Roarke. She wanted his children and his grandchildren. She wanted him to be there when she met her brother Jake and her sister. She wanted him there when the building inspector signed off on the final inspection of her skyscraper.

But how could she set things right?

Beside her, Jake tensed. "We've got company."

His words yanked her back to immediate problems,

and her stomach tensed and knotted. Looking into the side mirror as he'd taught her, she spied a police car. "Did you ask the cops to escort us?"

"Carleton may have. I asked for FBI protection." He hesitated as if he expected her to fly off the handle. "Sorry, I should have told you. It slipped my mind."

"It's okay. You're doing your job, trying to protect me. I don't expect you to explain every little detail."

He shot her a look of approval that warmed her to her toes. Then he glanced in his mirror and frowned. "That blue sedan three cars back has also been tailing us for several minutes."

"What's going on?"

He evaded her question. "Let's make sure I'm right before we jump to conclusions." Roarke swung a left, another left and then a third, circling the block. The cop and the sedan both followed.

"Are these the good guys or the bad guys?" Alexandra asked. Since everyone worked for a government agency, she found the situation confusing.

"Suspect everyone." Roarke turned off the road that hugged the coast and headed west toward the city. "There's no telling who leaked the information about our meeting with Viper. It could have been the cryptologist himself or someone monitoring his communications, or someone in ops could have bugged his office."

Roarke picked up his cell phone and dialed. She didn't want to distract him by asking questions, but she wondered whom he would call. "Did you get me air support?"

Air support? It sounded as if Roarke didn't think they could outrun the trouble behind them.

Alexandra tried to swallow, but her mouth was sand-dry with fear. Beside her, Roarke was all business, his gaze monitoring the road behind them, to the left and right, too.

As they headed onto a bridge that spanned the intracoastal waterway, Roarke wove in and out of traffic. But not fast enough.

The bridge master sounded the clangs and flashed lights that signaled traffic to stop so tall-masted sailboats could pass under the bridge. Only she couldn't see any sailboat or tugboat. In fact, she saw no reason at all for the bridge to be opening. When the car just in front of them stopped at the lowering barricade, Roarke slammed on the brakes.

"Get out. We'll try to cross on foot."

Alexandra's hands shook as she unfastened her seat belt, grabbed the blueprint tube and her purse. Roarke had leaped over the hood and practically yanked her out of her seat before she'd taken a breath.

"Come on! Come on!"

Cars and trucks on both sides of the bridge had stopped. But the bridge mechanism hadn't yet begun to open the bridge. If they hurried, they might cross to the other side on foot and avoid their pursuers.

Roarke glanced over his shoulder once, but Alexandra kept her eyes focused straight ahead. She didn't dare risk slowing Roarke down and forced her feet to move faster.

Then the bridge started to tilt upward beneath their feet. She would have gone back, but Roarke tugged her forward. "We can make it."

Alexandra put all her energy into running the last ten feet uphill. She slipped. Roarke yanked her to her feet and then pushed her. They reached the rising peak, the place where one side of the bridge separated from the other.

''Come on. Don't look down at the water. Just spot your landing on the other side,'' Roarke encouraged her.

It was only a foot or two and Alexandra jumped over the intracoastal waterway far below, grateful she'd never been afraid of heights. Roarke made the leap with her, never letting go of her hand.

Now on the other side of the bridge, they were running downhill, slipping and sliding and trying to reach the bottom and level pavement before the bridge opened wider and spilled them head over heels.

She wouldn't have remained upright without Roarke's steady support. Her chest heaved as her burning lungs fought for air. She wanted to celebrate their success, but one glance at Roarke's acute wariness, and she knew he didn't think they were in the clear.

Already, the bridge had started to close, the metal spans reversing direction. By running, they'd gained a head start. But they were now on foot, those chasing them in cars.

Just when Alexandra thought things couldn't possibly get worse, she heard the hum of a helicopter. In front of them two men exited their vehicles, weapons in hand.

She and Roarke couldn't go forward. They couldn't go back, since more men with guns waited behind them.

Before she could blink, Roarke was moving, pulling her toward the bridge's railing. He'd taken his weapon out of his pocket and aimed it at the two men approaching.

"What do we do?" she asked, wishing for her own weapon.

"We have no choice. Jump!"

Chapter Fifteen

"Jump?" She looked back over her shoulder. While the bridge was still closing, the two halves remained at least twenty feet apart. No way could she clear that distance—not even with a running start.

"Over the side." The urgency in Roarke's voice started her feet moving closer to the railing. "Into the water."

Oh, God.

He wanted her to jump off the bridge.

Oh, God.

While she didn't have an unusual fear of heights, any normal person would balk. She didn't want to parachute out of airplanes, join a high-wire act at the circus or jump off the damn bridge.

Yet Roarke would never have asked it of her if he'd believed they had another option. Holding the tube of blueprints tightly in her hand, Alexandra hurried the last steps to the railing, looked down and wet her lips. Judging heights wasn't her specialty, but they had to be at least five stories above the water. The impact...

Oh, God, the impact...

She recalled that moment back at the spring right

before she and Roarke had jumped into the water. He'd held her hand then and she imagined him holding it now, which was easy to do, since he was never far from her thoughts, always close to her heart.

She didn't question Roarke's judgment. She maneuvered one leg over the rail, then the other, pretending he was making the leap by her side.

"Now," he yelled.

And she let go.

Her stomach seemed to rise into her throat as the rest of her plunged.

And plunged.

Picking up speed.

Wind roaring in her ears.

The fall took forever. Went by too fast.

Her feet smacked the water. The force of the landing ripped the blueprint tube from her hand, twisted her arm, smacked one cheek until her ears rang.

Dark, briny water surrounded her.

She heard a boom, felt pressure and wondered dizzily if a bomb had gone off, then slowly realized Roarke must have landed in the water nearby. She kept plummeting deeper into the water. She had instinctively held her breath, but already felt the need for air.

At this depth, her eardrums started to hurt. She could barely see sunlight on the surface. Her shoes and clothing weighed her down.

Bubbles escaped from her mouth and she suddenly knew she wouldn't make it to the surface. She lacked the strength to fight through all that water weighing her down, lacked the air to make her arms and legs pull and kick.

ROARKE HAD LUNGED over the side the instant Alexandra had jumped. He'd focused on her in the air and started angling toward her the moment he struck water.

Fear made him use up his oxygen, but he knew one thing for certain. He wasn't coming up without her. No way would he lose another woman he loved.

Frantic, he felt around for her, forced himself deeper. His hand moved into some grass and he almost pulled away.

Not grass. Alexandra's hair.

He reached for her hand, found her shoulder. Terror shot through him at her lack of movement. Had she landed on her side? Busted her insides? Snapped her neck as Sydney had?

No.

Panic had him yanking her to the surface, kicking with all his strength, hoping his long swims in the spring would give him the power and stamina to overcome his dizziness and need for oxygen.

The light overhead grew brighter, but his vision blurred to two narrow tunnels. He kept going through sheer determination. Alexandra wouldn't drown. Not on his watch. Not ever. She was going to live to be an old lady and he would be there to watch her mellow.

Roarke's head broke the surface and he gasped for air. Overhead, he heard a gun battle. And the helicopter hovered directly over the bridge. Apparently Carleton and the cavalry had arrived.

Beside him, he propped Alexandra's face out of the water. She looked too white, her eyes glazed, and he was sure she'd stopped breathing. He couldn't do mouth-to-mouth while treading water; he had to get her to shore. But he'd come up in the damn middle of a very wide section of the intracoastal. Even if he could make it to shore with her, she'd be dead long before they arrived.

Holding her head between his hands, he kicked with all his strength and breathed air into her parted lips. Again he sucked air into his own lungs, then blew into her mouth, knowing her nostrils should be closed, knowing he wasn't doing it right but he needed three hands, two to keep her head up, one to close her nose. "Breathe for me. Breathe. Breathe. Breathe."

No response.

He twisted her in the water until her back rested against his chest, her head lolling on his shoulder. Placing his hands around her rib cage, he squeezed, performing a modified Heimlich maneuver.

He heard a slight cough. Her body shuddered and then she spit water out of the side of her mouth.

Thank God.

She was going to be okay. She hadn't been without oxygen long enough to suffer brain damage.

"You hurt anywhere?" he asked, still concerned over internal injuries from the force of smacking the water.

Dazed, she moved weakly. "I'm just tired. So tired."

"Hang on sweetheart, and I'll get you out of here."

He didn't know how he'd fulfil his promise. He looked up at the bridge, hoping to flag down help. He'd drifted from their position directly underneath and he could see men taking cover behind cars. Men shooting. Those in the chopper raining down bullets, right in the middle of civilian traffic.

Suddenly Roarke spied a familiar silhouette, hanging over the railing searching the water. And a bald man coming up fast behind him. Top Dog!

"Carleton! Behind you."

Carleton spun, ducked and threw Top Dog off the bridge. Then he leaped over the side of the bridge himself. Seconds later, he popped to the surface and swam over to Alexandra, leaving Roarke free to swim to where he'd seen Top Dog plunge beneath the water.

Top Dog surfaced almost next to Roarke with his weapon in his hand. Roarke knew the gun hadn't been in the water long enough to prevent the bullets from firing.

While Carleton and Alexandra swam away toward the bridge piling, Roarke lunged for Top Dog's weapon. The gun discharged but Roarke threw off his aim by smacking his wrist.

Top Dog dropped his gun and lunged, his hands clasped around Roarke's throat. The bald man might have twenty years on Roarke, but he also outweighed him by forty pounds. Forty pounds of muscle.

Roarke concentrated on finding the man's pinky, then bent it straight back until he felt the bone snap. Top Dog let out a screech underwater and bubbles of air emerged from his mouth.

Still Top Dog didn't let go of Roarke's throat. Roarke's lungs burned and he badly needed air. He jammed a foot into Top Dog's stomach and reached for the gun in his ankle holster at the same time. But he'd lost the gun during the plunge into the intercoastal.

Desperate for air, Roarke slammed a knee into Top Dog's chin. He caught the stronger man by surprise and snapped his neck. Roarke yanked the dead man's fingers from his throat and clawed his way to the surface. Gasping for air, he searched for Alexandra and Carleton, spotted them by the bridge piling and swam over.

"We're okay," Carleton assured him.

Alexandra swam beside Carleton, and she appeared to have recovered some strength. Roarke hoped the only damage she'd suffered was having the wind knocked out of her. She was mostly swimming on her own, but he noted that Carleton kept her within arm's reach.

Carleton shook his head. "If you hadn't warned me about Baldy... You saved my life again, thanks."

"What's going on up there?" Roarke asked, his throat a little raspy from the abuse he'd taken.

Carleton trod water and gave his report as if standing in his office. "We finally got some interdepartmental cooperation. At the FBI's request, the CIA traced the phone calls from that phone booth to a man who was running an unauthorized and highly illegal covert operation within the CIA."

"You identified Top Dog?" Roarke asked.

"Yep. Your Mr. Baldy was in charge of the men you killed in the warehouse and also the sniper back at the construction site."

"He's dead," Roarke muttered darkly.

Carleton tilted his head. "I believe he was driving the blue sedan that was tailing you."

"But why?" Alexandra asked, proving to Roarke that her muscles might be a little waterlogged, but her brain was firing on all cylinders.

"Once we decode your—"

"The papers!" Alexandra shook her head back and forth and let out a sob of frustration. "I lost them when I jumped into the water. Do you think the cardboard tube might float?"

They searched, but didn't find a thing. And when the chopper lowered a line, Roarke insisted that she climb inside the chopper to safety. The papers didn't matter. She could get another copy from her brother. Besides, everyone in the coverup was dead. According to Carleton, the entire cell was wiped out.

ALEXANDRA WRAPPED a blanket around herself, but what she really wanted were Roarke's arms to keep her warm. Carleton came up out of the water and into the chopper next, then finally Roarke. Ten minutes later, the chopper landed at the hospital where all of them declined medical treatment.

A joint FBI-CIA debriefing team met them, and they had to tell their story repeatedly. The worst part for Alexandra was being separated from Roarke. She had something to tell him. Something much more important than figuring out a twenty-something-year-old secret from her past.

Finally, hours and hours later, at Roarke's insistence, the debriefing team released her. He claimed there was no longer a rush to solve the mystery. The copy given away on her apartment doorstep had been destroyed by a rogue agent before he killed himself. Everyone involved seemed to be dead and the secret lost in the water and buried with them—except for the original her brother Jake had.

She didn't want to think about her brother or the past. She wanted to concentrate on her future. Especially one that included Roarke. He'd saved her life again today, but she'd learned something very important about herself, and she couldn't wait to tell him.

She wanted to be alone with him. Carleton offered to take them home. But she didn't want to face the mess of her apartment just yet.

"Can we go camping?" she asked with a mischievous glance at Roarke. She had her own man to love, and she intended to do everything in her power to keep him.

Even now, his handsome features stole her breath away—the arrogant chin, those piercing blue eyes that challenged her, dared her to take a flying leap at love.

And she did love him.

"Take us to Green Cove Springs," Roarke agreed, his lips curling upward into a smile of anticipation.

While Alexandra fully intended to track down her brother Jake, he should be safe with Top Dog dead. She'd waited years to meet her brother—another few days wouldn't matter. Days that she and Roarke could spend together, camping and sunning and loving under the stars.

But he couldn't be as impatient to be alone as she was, not when she was bursting to tell him about her epiphany. Finally Carleton dropped them off, promising to have a vehicle delivered tomorrow. Alexandra wasn't in any rush to leave the private playground. Her building had a few days before the inspectors would allow her crews to begin fixing the destruction.

In the meantime, she had her own fixing to do. With Roarke.

As soon as Carleton spun away, she turned into his arms and kissed him, hungry for the taste of him, knowing she'd never tire of his touch, his taste or the toughness that had seen her through the most trying time of her life.

"I love you," she admitted without the slightest doubt or the slightest hesitation.

Pain and passion battled in his eyes. "And I love you…"

It should have been an exhilarating moment, yet her excitement was tempered by the surety that a "but" would follow his declaration of love.

"…but you don't trust me."

"Yes, I do." And then she explained what she'd been waiting all day to say. "I jumped off that bridge when you asked me to."

"Yes, you did."

"I jumped without second-guessing you. Without question. And since then I've finally realized that if I could blindly put my life in your hands, surely I can trust you with my heart."

He held his hands along both her cheeks, tipping her head back to look into her eyes. "You're sure?"

"Oh, yes. Now stop wasting time and kiss me."

Epilogue

Above the streets of Washington, on the fifteenth floor
of the CIA building, an official frowned at the message
he'd anxiously awaited.

Files destroyed. Agents dead.

All of them? All dead? Reeling at the bad news, the
official worked on automatic pilot, dropping the doc-
ument into an ashtray and setting a match to it, watching it burn, knowing his plans were going up in flames
as well. While the mission had been successful, the
cost had been high.

Thirty years the team had been together, watching
one another's backs, keeping their vows of secrecy.
And even while the agent mourned, he took pride that
no one had talked. No one had ever betrayed the cell.

But the cost…

After the flames did their work, the agent poured
acid from a vase on his desk over the ashes to ensure
no one could ever read the message.

Too many old colleagues had died, but the man who

looked out over Washington shrugged. Everyone was expendable. Even loyal men could be replaced.

With both the original and the copy destroyed, he'd bought himself a margin of safety. But he couldn't rest. Not until the very last copy was found and destroyed.

This last sister was proving as resourceful as her difficult siblings. But she couldn't compete with his resources, his technology. All the siblings would be found, the final copies destroyed.

If anyone dared stand in his way, he'd destroy them. Just like all the others....

*   *   *   *   *

We hope you enjoyed

HIDDEN HEARTS,

Book II of Susan Kearney's new
Harlequin Intrigue series,

HIDE AND SEEK.

Please look for Book III,

LOVERS IN HIDING, HI #644 (12/01),

next month.
For a sneak preview of
LOVERS IN HIDING,
turn the page...

Prologue

Clay Rogan had never before been ordered into the office of the Director of Operations of the CIA. Although he worked daily at the imposing building in McLean, Virginia, the prospect of meeting the director had him curious and edgy. The legendary director was responsible for all covert operations—far from Clay's normal turf in cryptology.

After the D.O. had left an urgent message in the Hot Inbox file on Clay's computer, Clay had hoped he wasn't about to be transferred to another division. He loved his work. He loved solving puzzles and breaking codes, and while his six-foot-six frame made him seem more suited for active pursuits, nothing provided him with as much pleasure as giving his brain a good workout. A ride on his motorcycle came in only a close second. Although Clay had trained at the renowned farm in Camp Peary with the other recruits, he led a relatively normal life. He worked in an office, in front of a computer screen, scrutinizing bursts of satellite transmissions in an attempt to decode messages sent by foreign agents' transmitters.

As a master in his field, Clay had worked his way

up from rookie and whiz kid to running the show. Early on, his superiors had recognized his intuitive knack for breaking code by spotting patterns where others could not. He'd earned the nickname Viper when he'd broken a Chinese code involving snakelike curves that had mystified other experts for years.

But going into the field was as far-fetched an idea to Clay as dogs barking in Morse code. Sure, he'd taken the same basic courses required of all the other operatives—explosives detection, surveillance and countersurveillance, shooting a variety of weapons, and running counterintelligence, counter narcotics and paramilitary operations—but those activities were far outside his area of expertise.

So he had no idea why he'd been ordered to the D.O.'s office. Under normal circumstances he'd hesitate to intrude into the ultra-secret fifteenth floor, but the message in his Hot file this morning had left him no alternative.

He was to report to the D.O. himself. And tell no one.

Highly unusual. Highly irregular. Orders normally came down through channels.

The moment Clay arrived, the D.O.'s secretary ushered him into the opulent office. Although he'd never met the head of one of the most important government departments, he'd seen the director on television many times, reporting to Congress and briefing the Senate.

Up close, Mr. Lionel Barret's bulldog face looked even more aggressive than on the little screen. Yet, the moment Clay entered, he graciously rose and came around his desk to shake hands, his spit-shined shoes squeaking.

"Thank you for coming so promptly."

Clay saw no reason to respond to the polite comment. Both men knew he hadn't been given a choice. When the director commanded, CIA employees obeyed with an extra snap in their steps, not just because the director was in charge; the man was famous for turning more foreign spies into double agents than any other operative in the Agency's long and convoluted history.

The hand that grasped Clay's had short, ragged nails, bitten down low on the fingertips. The palm was hard, cool and powerful. The director gestured for Clay to sit and then, surprisingly, pulled up a chair beside him, a friendly action that made Clay even more wary.

"I'm sure you're curious as to why you're here, so I'll get right to the point." Barret's puppy-dog eyes peered at Clay with a hopeful expression. "I'd like your help in a little matter."

Little? The D.O. didn't involve himself in *little* matters. He left that for underlings. But Clay kept his expression neutral. "Yes, sir?"

"Almost thirty years ago, a married couple worked for the Agency. Both of them were operatives. The woman was killed and her husband died in a mysterious car accident a short time later. Three of their children survived, and the Agency hired a lawyer to find homes for the kids. Those children are now adults. I believe they're in danger."

"Sir?" Was the D.O. asking Clay to protect them? That was so far from his area of expertise, he had trouble believing that someone who had access to his file would have chosen him for the job.

"The eldest is a man named Jake Cochran. Ever heard of him?"

"Should I have, sir?"

"Jake grew up in foster homes. When he graduated from high school he tracked down the attorney we hired decades ago and tried to find his sisters."

"The kids were split up? I thought family services tries to keep them together."

"But then they would have been easier to track. And since we feared for their safety, it was decided that the kids would be separated." Barret paused. "The parents were damn fine operatives, the best, so it's not surprising that Jake Cochran established one of the premier detective agencies in Florida. All the while, he kept searching for his sisters.

"Did he find them, sir?"

"He will."

Clay frowned. "I don't understand, sir."

He didn't like the idea of children being separated. Families should stick together, and he sincerely hoped the D.O. didn't want him to have anything to do with keeping the siblings apart.

"Jake found adoption records with his sisters' new names and addresses. He mailed them each a letter with old photographs and copies of his mother's papers. He also hired bodyguards to protect his sisters."

Clay put the pieces together quickly. "The siblings are in danger because of the mother's documents?"

"You catch on quick. Jake and one sister have already gone underground. I want you to befriend the second sister, get her to trust you."

"Am I permitted to know why?"

Barret's chuckled. "Absolutely. I need you to decode the documents."

Clay finally understood why he'd been chosen for this mission. His hobby was deciphering old codes like the one the special agent might have used almost thirty years ago—information that was most assuredly right in his file along with his favorite flavor of chewing gum, cherry; his preferences in women, model-thin blondes with small, high breasts and cool intelligence; and his favorite leather jacket size—extra large.

Still he was reluctant to take on the full assignment. Although he itched to try his luck with the old codes, protection wasn't his specialty and he didn't want to get someone killed. "Sir, surely there are people much more qualified than me to protect the sister—"

"Melinda Murphy."

"To protect Ms. Murphy—"

"But you're the best-qualified cryptologist for the job." The D.O. gave him a significant look. Clay didn't have to know the man well to understand that he was expected to keep his mouth shut, his orders committed to memory. But why hadn't the D.O. assigned another more qualified agent to protect the woman and allowed Clay to do what he did best— decode? Was he missing something? Or was he just annoyed because he didn't yet have all the pieces to the puzzle? After a taut silence, the D.O. finally added, "We don't want to alert anyone else to the situation."

We? So now it was a team effort. But it would be Clay's ass on the line, and the girl's, too, if he screwed up. "May I ask why *we* are keeping this operation to just us, sir?"

His expertise wouldn't come into play until later,

after he'd gained the woman's trust, and Clay hoped he wouldn't be asked to betray her in order to bring the code to the Agency. Despite his credentials as a fully-trained operative, he didn't like lies.

"Because I suspect someone inside the CIA is running their own secret operation against these siblings."

Clay swallowed hard, suddenly understanding the covert nature of this extremely dangerous assignment. No wonder the D.O. wanted him to work alone—less chance of a leak. And a leak could be critical, since his job was to ferret out a traitor within the CIA.

"Do I—"

"No backup. No partners. Just you with a direct phone line to me."

"And my current assignments?"

"I'll handle that. You take care of the woman, Viper. Melinda Murphy lives in Daytona Beach, Florida." The director handed him a file. "Just find her, decode the papers and bring the results back to me. Only to me."

'TIS THE SEASON FOR...

HARLEQUIN®
INTRIGUE®

Fill your Christmas stocking with
two new seasonal tales of breathtaking
romantic suspense from a couple
of your favorite authors.

ANOTHER WOMAN'S BABY
Joanna Wayne
(11/01)

A WOMAN WITH A MYSTERY
B.J. Daniels
(12/01)

Available at your favorite retail outlet.

HARLEQUIN®
Makes any time special ®

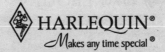

TRUE BLOOD, TEXAS

Coming in December 2001...

THE COWBOY'S SECRET SON

by

Gayle Wilson

Lost:

His first love. Mark Peterson had never forgotten Jillian Salvini, whose family had left town in the middle of the night so many years ago.

Found:

Her son's father. Jillian has finally returned... with her son, Drew, who bears an uncanny resemblance to Jillian's next-door neighbor: Mark Peterson!

Can old wounds and past betrayals be overcome, so that Mark, Jillian and Drew can finally become a family?

Finder's Keepers: bringing families together

HARLEQUIN®
Makes any time special®

Visit us at www.eHarlequin.com

TBTCNM4

Welcome to

Silhouette

DREAMSCAPES...

a world where passion and danger mingle
together...and the temptation of dark,
sensual romance awaits.

In December 2001,
look for these four
alluring romances:

FROM A DISTANCE
by Emilie Richards

THE PERFECT KISS
by Amanda Stevens

SEA GATE
by Maura Seger

**SOMETHING
BEAUTIFUL**
by Marilyn Tracy

*Available at
your favorite retail outlet.*

Where love comes alive™

Visit Silhouette at www.eHarlequin.com   RCDREAM4

Two very different heroes. Two very different stories.
One gripping and passionate reading experience!

NIGHT AND DAY

A unique 2-in-1 from

HARLEQUIN®

INTRIGUE®

featuring editorially connected stories by:

ANNE
STUART

and

GAYLE WILSON

Michael Blackheart and Duncan Cullen are as
different as NIGHT AND DAY. Yet they share a goal—
and neither man can imagine the dark world that
such a quest will take them on.

Available in November 2001 at your favorite retail outlet.

HARLEQUIN®
Makes any time special ®

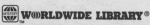